# PHOENIX RISING

# PHOENIX RISING

Or How to Survive Your Life

## CYNTHIA D. GRANT

ATHENEUM   1989   NEW YORK

Copyright © 1989 by Cynthia D. Grant

Atheneum
Macmillan Publishing Company
866 Third Avenue, New York, NY 10022
Collier Macmillan Canada, Inc.
First Edition
Printed in the United States of America
10  9  8  7  6  5  4  3  2  1

Designed by Barbara A. Fitzsimmons

Library of Congress Cataloging-in-Publication Data
Grant, Cynthia D.
Phoenix rising: or how to survive your life/Cynthia D. Grant.—1st ed.   p.   cm.
Summary: Helen's death at eighteen from cancer shatters the lives of her parents and siblings, especially her younger sister, Jessie, who tries to cope with her feelings of pain and confusion by reading pages from Helen's diary.
ISBN 0-689-31458-2
[1. Death—Fiction.   2. Cancer—Fiction.   3. Family problems—Fiction.]   I. Title.   II. Title: How to survive your life.
PZ7.G76672Ph   1989
[Fic]—dc19
88-7370   CIP   AC

*For Jane, John W., Jody, John,*
    *Quinn,*
    *Brian,*
    *Paulette Kizzar,*
    *Katie,*
    *Hayyet,*
    *and, as always,*
*for my sister, Princess Al*

The earth is your mother,
She holds you.
The sky is your father,
He protects you.
Rainbow is your sister,
she loves you.
The winds are your brothers,
they sing to you.
Sleep,
sleep,
We are together always
We are together always
There never was a time
when this
was not so.

*Navajo lullaby*

# PHOENIX RISING

―――――――――――――――――――――――――――     I

WE ARE IN THE COUNTRY, HELEN AND I, IN A BEAUTIFUL,
boundless field. The birds are making a joyous racket and
it's autumn. The sky is so blue!

We're laughing. Helen's telling a funny story. I can't hear
the words but I know her thoughts. She's more like my twin
than my big sister.

But something's wrong. The world is tilting. It's hard to
stand up. I say, "Helen, what's happening?" and she smiles
and says, "Don't worry; it's only an earthquake."

Earthquake! The ground beneath me buckles, roaring
and ripping apart. I'm falling, falling. . . . Then everything
changes; the field is smoothly seamed again, the sun is warm,
the birds are singing—but Helen has disappeared. I run in
wild circles, crying, "Helen, where are you?" realizing, my
heart cracking open, that the earth has swallowed her. Helen
is gone.

Dr. Shubert says, "You understand what this dream means, don't you, Jessie. Your sister has gone into the ground."

Helen's ashes were scattered three months ago, in the grove at Foothill Park where we loved to go, just beyond that beautiful field.

Mom and Dad wanted Lucas and me to go with them, but as usual, Lucas disappeared. And I . . . just couldn't. I stayed at home in our—my—room.

Helen doesn't exist anymore, except in the past and in my mind. No matter how long I wait, I'll never see her again. It's a hard idea to get used to.

Oh, Helen. I can't get used to it.

People say I'm doing well, handling the situation beautifully; as if they'd thought, when she died five months ago, that I was going to die, too.

I thought I would. I wanted to.

But sadness doesn't kill you.

When people ask how you are, they want you to say fine. They think you're doing swell if you tell jokes. The worse things get, the funnier I am. It's like being a comedian on the *Titanic*. *Folks, do you ever get that sinking feeling? But seriously, doesn't the band sound terrific?*

You and Helen were so close, people say.

Hearing that past tense kills me.

Dr. Shubert says I have to get on with my life. Jessie, you must pick up the pieces. . . . Sometimes things break so badly, they shatter, and the pieces are too small to gather up again.

One week after Helen died, I woke up in the night. The room was luminous with moonlight spilling onto Helen's bed, the blankets flat, the pillow empty. The curtains were moving. Helen's dead, they whispered. She's dead and she's never coming back.

I felt my heart break, and the pain almost killed me. Then, for a long time, I didn't feel anything.

My best friend by default, Bambi Sue Bordtz, said I wasn't crying enough.

"Geez, Jess, you're acting so weird," she said. "When my cousin died, I cried my eyes out and I didn't even like him. If I had a sister and she died, I couldn't stand it."

Did anybody ask me if I could stand it? Did anyone give me a choice?

A lot of our friends have quit talking about Helen. They think they're being kind. They act as if she'd never existed, as if I'd imagined my eighteen-year-old sister. They erase her like that, again and again: Helen who?

It's worse with new people. "Do you have any brothers or sisters?" they ask. When I have to tell them my sister's dead, they look scared, as if they're afraid I might cry; then apologize, as though it were their fault. She dies in their eyes and that's how they'll always see her.

Helen was the most alive person I knew.

My brother hates to talk about Helen. When I mention her, he changes the subject, or plays his guitar extra loud, or splits. Dad's almost as bad. When Mom talks about Helen, he gets all sad—as if Helen was a tragedy. As if her whole life was her death. He plays a lot of golf lately, when it's not raining, or even when it is. He quit asking Lucas to go with him a long time ago. Lucas can't see the game at all. Follow the bouncing ball, he says. Then Dad makes a crack about Lucas's music, and the next thing you know, they're yelling and screaming—

I go into my room and shut the door. Since Helen died, it seems like people are always leaving and doors are closing.

Sometimes I get so sick of the arguments I wish Lucas would move out, but he can't afford his own place. The record store where he works pays minimum wage and his music gigs aren't steady. Then I worry: When Lucas moves out, will we see him anymore? Will he disappear like Helen?

It's stupid to worry so much. Nothing I can do about it, anyway.

Bloomfield called me today; this jerk that Helen went out with for a while. Then he found out she had cancer (thanks to Bambi Sue Bigmouth) and he told Helen he couldn't see her anymore; she was getting "too intense"; he "needed space."

"As if I cared!" Helen said. But I know she did, though she pretended it didn't matter. He dumped her like a ton of bricks, then had the gall to call me up. I said I wouldn't go out with him if he was the last jerk on the face of the earth, and was going to say a lot more but he hung up on me.

When I told Bambi about it, she said, "No wonder you don't have any boyfriends, Jess! Beggars can't be choosers." If Bambi's not here, driving me crazy in person, she's phoning to announce that nothing's new. At least she doesn't call me from the john anymore. Don't ever do that again, I said. You have to be direct with Bambi. A right cross to the jaw would only be a subtle hint.

She wants me to go shopping with her tomorrow. If shopping were an Olympic event, Bambi would be a gold medalist. In third grade, when we got our library cards, she thought we were charging the books. She has credit cards at Bullocks, Macy's, the Emporium, Saks, and Neiman Marcus. Her dad just gave her a convertible for her birthday. I couldn't believe it; he doesn't even like her. "They wanted me, so they have to give me what I want," Bambi says. "I didn't ask to be born."

It wasn't so bad when Helen was here. We spread Bambi around. We shared her. Now I'm supposed to cheer her up all the time and I can't even save myself. I'm sinking. But I can't tell the folks; they're treading water themselves, and Lucas is never here. Even if he were, I couldn't tell him what I'm thinking.

If only I could talk to Helen. That's how I felt when she died; I could survive it if I could talk to Helen.

That was the catch.

I'm supposed to be able to talk to Dr. Shubert, but she was my age in 1938. Dad wanted Lucas to see her, too, but he refused. Nobody can make Lucas do anything. When he was six he got lost; the cops turned out and half the city was looking for him. When they found him in a tree, five miles from home, he wasn't scared, he wasn't relieved.

He said, "I knew where I was all the time."

Dr. Shubert's trying to help me get rid of the dreams. It's gotten so bad I can't stand to fall asleep. The lids go down but my eyes stay open, and on the thin, pink screens I see Helen.

Last night the two of us were in the car, Helen driving. The radio was loud, the way she liked it, playing something hard and fast. We were going to the ocean. We were almost there. I smelled seaweed baking in the sun.

Then no one was driving. Helen was gone. I turned around and she was standing by the side of the road. The brakes wouldn't work; I couldn't stop the car. It carried me far away. In the distance, Helen got tinier and tinier.

I didn't mean to leave her behind.

I don't want to dream. I want to fall asleep and wake up ten years from now. I'll be twenty-seven and Lucas will be thirty—and Helen will still be eighteen.

Helen. All those years; all that learning, changing, growing. She had to have braces on her teeth. Why? What was the point? This was always going to happen; it was lying ahead and we didn't even know it. We went right on living, laughing, hoping. We were so stupid.

Someone's touching my knee. Someone's talking to me. "Jessie," Dr. Shubert says, "I can't help if you won't tell me what you're thinking."

"There really isn't much to say," I answer.

No one can help me. No one is my sister.

## 2

BAMBI SAYS, "AT LEAST IT WASN'T A BIG SHOCK. YOU KNEW she was going to die."

Everybody knows they're going to die, but nobody believes it. Death is always a big shock. And Bambi is always a birdbrain.

They found the first tumor when Helen was fourteen. Sometimes she was better, sometimes worse. The cancer just became part of her life. We never admitted that it might kill her. Once you let an idea like that into your mind, it's as if you're agreeing, as if you're saying yes, and we had to keep saying no, no, no—

Right after she died I was scared I'd turn on the TV one night and see scientists hugging each other and screaming: "Eureka! We've found the cure!"

It would be too late—too late for Helen. What difference would it make if all those strangers got saved?

I was ashamed of the way I was thinking.

Helen was such an unlikely statistic. Being sick wasn't her idea. Next to her picture in the high school yearbook, it doesn't say: *Plans to be a cancer victim.* In the picture her hair is still shiny and thick, her eyes are smiling, her cheeks are round. . . .

At the end, she was so thin. Helen had to die; she was so ill there was nowhere else to go.

She didn't talk about the cancer much. Neither did we; it wasn't a dinner table topic. When she did bring it up, I'd skirt the subject; like this time she and I were picnicking at Foothill Park last spring. The meadow by the lake was orange with poppies, and the air was so sweet you tasted flowers.

Helen said, "I'm so sick of being sick. I wish I'd get better or just die."

"You won't die," I replied automatically. "You're just tired."

"I'm tired of being tired," she said. "This girl at the clinic died last week and she—"

"You won't die! Get morbid about it!" I shouted, and ran down to the lake.

I thought we had all the time in the world. I thought the cancer was a big mistake that would get straightened out any second.

It was hard to tell what was going on sometimes. The doctors were vague. And Mom and Dad didn't ask a lot of tough questions. Maybe they knew they'd hate the answers. If there were answers. Doctors aren't psychics. Nobody knows what's going to happen. Dr. Yee said it was important to remain optimistic, that a positive attitude is part of any cure. So we all kept pretending that everything was fine—

One second Daddy's carrying Helen out to the car. The next thing you know, it's the following morning and he and Mom are walking in the door. They didn't say anything, but Lucas and I knew. The moment is frozen in my mind: all of us standing there, looking at each other.

Helen slipped through our fingers like a sunny day. We'd thought it would be summer forever.

Why didn't God take me instead? I am such a *creep* compared to Helen.

Answer: because that big, blue sky is as empty as a promise. We're all down here on our own, alone, trying not to bump into the furniture.

My attitude stinks. This is not a new development. Helen claimed I was a wise guy from birth; more like a midget than a kid. Where she saw rainbows, I saw puddles. Look on the bright side, Jess!

Where's the bright side now, Helen? You took it with you when you left.

I'm supposed to sit for these kids she used to watch. Helen played games with them and read them stories. I keep them from killing each other and watch TV. The little girl asks me, "When's Helen coming back?" Sara Rose is six and she doesn't get death; she's only seen it in the cartoons on TV. The steam-rollered cat springs back to life. "Where's Helen?" Sara Rose asks, and it makes me want to scream. I shouldn't baby-sit; I'm no good with kids, but I can use the money.

What for? I can't think of anything I want anymore. Not clothes or makeup or tapes. It's all so much blahblah. Including school. I have *got* to start paying attention in class or I'll never graduate in June. It's all so pointless. Who cares about math? All you need to know is how to subtract. Take away one from five equals none.

My family is going down the drain.

Dr. Shubert has suggested a new way for the four of us to talk to each other so we can be sure we understand what's being said. She calls it the "playback" technique. This method is guaranteed to cut down on arguments and make any conversation take twice as long.

Old, unimproved dinner table conversation:

Mom: Eat more broccoli, honey.

Me: I'm not hungry.

Mom: I'm sorry. Did I overcook it?

Me: No! It's fine. I'm just not hungry.

Lucas: Can I use the car tonight?

Dad: Again?

Lucas: What do you mean, again?

Dad: You borrowed it last night.

Lucas: So? The Impala's on the fritz. I need to borrow it again.

Dad: Not if you take that attitude.

Mom: Bill—

Lucas: What's wrong with my attitude?

Mom: Lucas—

Dad: I might like to know where you're going.

Lucas: I'm not a baby! I'm twenty years old!

Mom: Can we all please lower our voices, please? Your father is just—

Lucas: (exiting) Forget it!

Dad: Come back here and apologize to your mother!


New, improved dialogue, using Dr. Shubert's "playback" technique:

Mom: Eat some more broccoli, honey.

Me: No thanks. I'm not hungry.

Mom: You're not hungry.

Me: No.

Mom: Oh.

Lucas: Can I use the car tonight?

Dad: You want to borrow the car.

Lucas: Yes. My car isn't working.

Dad: You borrowed it last night and you need to borrow it again.

Lucas: That's right. I need to go someplace.

Dad: Where?

Lucas: Out.

Dad: You need to go out.

Lucas: Yes.

Dad: Can you be more specific?

Lucas: You're saying that you want to know where I'm going.

Dad: That's correct. Can you be more specific?

Lucas: I'm not a baby! I'm twenty years old!

Mom: Lucas! Bill—

Dad: Don't take that tone with me!

Lucas: Don't you talk to my mother like that!

Dad: I was talking to you!

Mom: Will everybody please—

She's always in the middle, like a referee. No matter who wins, she loses.

Mom wants me to help her sort through Helen's things. Her blouses are still in the ironing basket. Her black boots are under the bed. I can wear some of her clothes but our styles are different. Helen is a V-necked-sweater type of person. I haven't worn a skirt since I was six.

We could've had our own rooms years ago, but I acted like a baby whenever Helen brought it up. It made me feel safe, when I woke up in the night, to hear Helen's soft breathing in the dark.

I've found her last diary. She always kept diaries. There's millions of them, at the top of her closet, and this one, started almost a year ago and kept in the nightstand by her bed.

I don't know if I should read it. I've never read her diaries—except for that one time Bambi and I sneaked a peek, years back. Helen was raving about this guy who sat in front of her in English. Mr. Wonderful, she called him. "So, how's Mr. Wonderful?" Bambi asked her, and Helen threw a fit.

But I'm tempted. Why was she writing stuff down on paper if she didn't want it to be read? She was always writing something; poems or stories. Her words are all I have left. I want to know what Helen was thinking, deep inside herself.

Sometimes when Lucas and the folks are gone, I go through the photograph albums, or I get out the projector and screen the family movies of us at home or on trips.

The movies are weird. Not much is happening. Mom and Dad are smiling and waving, or talking to the camera even though there's no sound. Lucas is usually scowling and straining to edge out of the frame, as if he's been kidnapped by an alien family and doesn't care for life on Mars. There's Helen as a baby, with fat pink arms, and later as a Brownie, her dark bangs clipped short.

Then there's me, Miss Spaghetti Legs. I look like a stick figure with hair, a tangled mass of long blond curls. I'm peering out of it as if it were a thicket. Lucas used to call me Cousin It.

Bambi says I should cut my hair. She says it makes me look like a kid.

I liked being a kid. I hate being like this. Nothing is familiar anymore. Mom and Dad aren't smiling. Lucas has escaped. My body's different, getting big and fat. (Dr. Shubert says I have a distorted self-image. I'm five feet eight and weigh a hundred and ten pounds.) I'm going to a shrink. This is my last year of high school.

Helen is gone and I'm alone.

I want her diary to talk to me, to say: *Don't worry, Jess. I'm still your big sister and I still love you the best. You can't see me anymore, but that doesn't mean I'm dead. It means—*

"Jessie? Jessie Castle?"

"Yes, Mrs. Smith?"

Startled, I lift my head, realizing that I'm supposed to have been reading the textbook on my desk.

Everyone in class is smiling at me. I'm the resident comedian. Poor Jessie, they say, she's had it pretty tough, but it's amazing how she's pulled her act together.

"Jessie, would you please tell us what you consider to be the gravest threat to public health?"

"Life," I say promptly. "Closely followed by death."

Everybody laughs. Then the bell rings and we all file out.

## 3

JANUARY 3

*The beginning of a brand new journal. The beginning of a brand new year. All those days and pages to fill!*

*I wonder who I'm writing to when I write in here.*

*When I was a kid I wrote KEEP OUT! in the front of all those little, fat diaries; the ones with a key you lose right away. Now I write ENTER AT YOUR OWN RISK, which is more like saying: Come In If You Must, But Watch Your Step.*

*Who is the You I'm speaking to? Me, I guess, so that later on I'll be able to remember what I was thinking about now; and to help me figure stuff out. That's partly it. I know what I'm thinking when I see it in print. But I must believe that someone else will read it, too; otherwise, why would I say Enter? (Years from now, when I'm a famous author, my biographer will say: "Helen Castle ate an ice-cream cone and washed her hair that day.")*

*Dream on.*

*Today Ms. Tormey read "The End" to the class; my story about the world blowing up in a nuclear blast. It's sappy but I love the last paragraph: "A quick flash and the sky was filled with orange light. It was almost like the sunset. Then it reached out its long, fiery fingers and stroked the fur of the kitten he held in his lap."*

*Nobody said a word when she was done. At times like that I can tell (dare I say it) that I'm a real writer; by the way the people listen and the way their faces change; as if the words had carried them to another, realer world inside their heads.*

*I really want to be published someday. Because when you write a story it's like talking to someone with your mind, and when somebody reads it, the two of you connect. Otherwise, it's like talking to yourself, or throwing a ball that nobody catches.*

*Blah blah blah. I'm so profound.*

*The other day Bambi told me the most amazing thing. When she was thirteen she got really depressed one night when her parents were out and she was all by herself. Totally down, like life was too awful to bear, and like she couldn't do anything right and never would.*

*So she rode her bike to the drugstore and bought a box of SleepEze and went home and took all of them, then lay down on her bed.*

*After awhile she got scared and she didn't want to die anymore, but she didn't know what to do. Her parents came home and she was afraid to tell them because she knew they'd hit the roof. So she just went to sleep and hoped for the best.*

*I'm the first person she's ever told, she said, because it sounds so stupid.*

*No it doesn't. It sounds sad.*

*Bloomfield came by tonight.*

*After he left, Mom said: "Doesn't Richard ever smile?"*

*At first I didn't know who she meant. Everybody except the teachers calls him by his last name.*

*Yeah, he smiles sometimes, I said. Usually when something's not funny. He's not the kind of guy who goes around grinning. Mostly he just smirks.*

*I don't know why I like him. We argue all the time. It's stupid, but we keep on doing it, like it's some kind of game we have to keep playing.*

*I don't know. He's not even good-looking. Well, yes he is, in a way. He has a good face (when he's not sneering) and all that curly hair. Too bad he's such a jerk.*

*Tonight he said: "Want to go out on Friday?"*

*Me: (surprised) "With you?"*

*Him: "No, with my father. Mom's out of town."*

*Why can't he just be nice? He's so sarcastic I end up being that way too, in self-defense. We've always got our dukes up.*

*I think I love him.*

*But I'm not sure because I don't know what that kind of love feels like. If it feels like wanting to kiss and sock him, wanting to hug him and push him down the stairs, sweet and prickly and happy and sad—*

*Then I love him.*

*He'd sure be thrilled to hear that.*

*Lucas keeps practicing the same song in his room, but it sounds like he's under this bed. It's a Beatles' song; I forget which one. He'd flip if I said that.*

*Too bad he wasn't a teenager in the sixties. That's when it was all happening, he says. It's like he got to the party after the band left. In my opinion, he'll never be happy. He's a perfectionist and the world is too screwed up. Nobody he knows takes music as seriously as he does. He's so good at it, he's always alone; he's out on the edge by himself. Maybe someday he'll find people who share that special place. Unless Dad kills him first. He'd better turn down that amp.*

*Jessie thinks Lucas is smoking dope, but he always acts so strange it's hard to tell.*

*I really like that big orange cat at the clinic. His name is Chemo and he's such a ham! The patients and staff stuff him with goodies so he's enormous, though lots of it is fluff. He's some kind of exotic breed; part pig, according to Dr. Yee.*

*I was telling Jess how much I like that cat, and she said, "Oh, they just have him there so the patients will forget what kind of place it is."*

*So? Anyway, that's not Chemo's fault. Jessie's in a bad mood lately. I try to talk with her, but she won't talk. Things get so tense around this house sometimes, it's crazy.*

*Part of it's me, I guess. But I'm feeling pretty good these days. I wish they wouldn't worry.*

*I forgot to mention that Bloomfield brought me a present: a can of smoked oysters. They tasted blue-gray. Some boys bring you flowers; Bloomfield brings fish.*

*Jessie says he's a pain in the drain.*

# 4

IN A SPONTANEOUS DISPLAY OF BROTHERLY AFFECTION (NO doubt brought on by my mother's tearful pleas), Lucas has agreed to Spend Time With Jessie.

The folks are concerned about me.

"You're too thin," my father says. "Too pale. You spend too much time in your room."

If I went out more, he'd say I was never home. My mother tries to feed me.

"Honey, wouldn't you like more steak?"

"No thanks. I'm stuffed."

"You've hardly touched your plate."

"It's too tough."

"The steak?" Tears brim in her eyes.

"The plate, I mean! Mom, I'm kidding!"

They want to take me on a trip over Christmas vacation. They've offered to buy me clothes. My dad's even talked about getting me a car. One tiny drawback: I don't know how to drive.

"It's easy, honey. I'll teach you."

He taught Helen and it almost drove her crazy: Watch out for that kid! That bus! That bike! There's a rumor going around that my brother will teach me, but when Lucas heard it, he just rolled his eyes.

He appeared in my bedroom doorway one night, after a long, loud discussion with my folks downstairs, in which my name came up repeatedly.

If I were a painter I'd frame Lucas in a doorway; always on the threshold, ready to leave.

"Want to go to a concert with me?" he asked.

I'd been sitting at my desk, pretending to study. I removed the pen from my mouth. "Who's playing?"

"B. B. King, at the Circle Star. I got tickets."

My father bought them. He knew Lucas would bite. The hook: He has to take me with him.

"All right," I said.

"Okay," he said.

So we drove up there on Saturday night, in Lucas's old white Impala, which he'd kind of fixed. The motor sounded like crazed chipmunks. Lucas's door won't open, so he climbed in the window.

It was cold but he kept his window unrolled and the night blew into the car. With anyone else you could say: Please close it—but Lucas makes the words freeze in my mouth. His moods shift so swiftly, from bad to worse, that we tend to treat him like a volatile mixture that could explode if it's not handled right.

Helen wasn't afraid of Lucas. She called him a spoiled brat.

He snapped on the radio, twirling the dial until he found Chuck Berry. He jacked up the volume till the speakers boomed, beating rhythm on the steering wheel with his wrists.

I sneaked looks at Lucas to see what girls see in him. He's tall and skinny with pale, crazy hair that would curl if it weren't so long. He has a soft, white mustache and a tiny beard. Now Dad can't say that Lucas looks like a girl. He flipped when Lucas pierced his ear with a tiny gold stud.

"What's the matter with you?" my father shouted. "Do you want people to think you're gay?"

"Hey!" Lucas said. "I don't care what people think! Including you!"

"That's obvious, from the way you dress!"

"At least I'm not a grayman like you!" "Grayman" is Lucas's word for anyone who, like our architect father, wears a suit to work.

They fight a lot more than they used to. Since Helen died, it's as if my father thinks that he won't cry as long as he keeps shouting. And my brother thinks—who knows what Lucas thinks? Sometimes I feel like I don't know him at all.

He finally noticed my hair blowing and rolled up the window halfway.

"Thanks."

"I hope we're not late," he said.

Suddenly I felt far from home, and alone. I wanted to feel close to my brother.

"I found Helen's diary," I said.

"Oh?" He stiffened like he always does at the mention of her name.

"I've been reading it."

"Why? You shouldn't," he said. "It's private."

"At the front it says it's okay."

"It says it's okay to read her diary?"

"It says 'Enter At Your Own Risk.' "

Lucas shook his head. "If she'd wanted you to read it, she wouldn't have hidden it."

"It wasn't exactly hidden." I felt like crying. It would be so good to talk about Helen. But Lucas won't talk; he acts disgusted.

"It makes me feel close to her," I said. "She's talking about her thoughts."

"You know what she thought."

"Not about everything. Helen was kind of a private person."

"Maybe she'd like to stay that way," he said.

We passed a highway sign with a fork painted on it, indicating an exit to a restaurant. A long time ago Lucas told Helen those signs meant we were coming to a fork in the road.

"Look at the traffic," he growled, taking the Circle Star

exit. Isn't he part of it? Does he expect his own lane? He likes to preach about the psychedelic sixties; how groovy they were, peace, love, and flowers. But behind the steering wheel, he acts just like Dad. Life's no joy ride; it's a trip to the dentist.

Lucas looked strange when he got out of the car; not only because he climbed out the window. He was dressed in black, plus a scarlet silk-lined cape, and midnight-colored shades. He looked like a cross between a hippie and a hit man. Most of the people looked elegant, and I wished I'd worn something special. I could've borrowed one of Helen's dresses.

We had really good seats, down front, on the aisle. The place filled up fast.

"I've always wanted to see B. B. He's the best," Lucas said. "And the opening act is good, too."

They played rhythm and blues. The music moved Lucas. As soon as it started he couldn't sit still. He drummed his fingers, tapped his toes.

"All right!" He applauded, his face shining in the dark, happier than I'd seen him in ages. I imagined the two of us going to other places, hearing music, seeing movies. The cold stone in my stomach dissolved.

Then it was time for B. B. King's band. We were close enough to really see their faces. They were older than the warm-up act and dressed in slick suits. They cruised through the intro, giving B. B. a big buildup.

The great man burst onstage. The crowd, including

Lucas, roared, giving him a standing ovation. He smiled and waved and began to play—then everything went wrong.

Instead of just playing and singing the blues, he hammed it up, he told jokes, he broke into fake sobs in the middle of one song until the audience howled with laughter.

Beside me, I could feel my brother burning.

"What is this, some Vegas revue?" he muttered. "I do not believe this."

B. B. waltzed around the stage, leading the audience in a round. "First the girls. Sing out," he said. "Now you boys."

As if that were a cue, Lucas leaped up. "Let's go." He flew up the dark aisle, me running to keep up with him, past the happy faces, through the brightly lit lobby, out into the parking lot—

"Lucas, why are we leaving?"

He looked at me as though he'd never heard such a stupid question in his life. "Where's the car?" he shouted.

"How should I know?"

When we found it, we didn't head home. Lucas drove toward San Francisco, raving.

"The man is dead but the show goes on! He's just going through the motions! Did you see that band? The zombie patrol! I'd be a junkie, too, if I had to listen to those jokes!"

"I thought he sounded good, Lucas."

"He's sold out the blues! The man is betraying everything that's made him great!"

We drove into the section of the city my father's warned

me against: bars, topless clubs, liquor stores, and knots of people standing on street corners, as if they were waiting for an accident to watch.

"Where are we going?"

"This club I know," Lucas said. Parking the Impala was like landing a whale.

The sign outside the club said you had to be twenty-one to enter, but nobody stopped us. The tiny, dark room was jammed with tables and faces, mostly black, and a thick layer of blue cigarette smoke.

Lucas moved toward the makeshift stage, where a band was playing, me trailing him like a shadow. He leaned against the wall next to a man with yellow eyes. The man looked Lucas over leisurely, lingering on his protest button. It's from the sixties. It says STOP THE WAR.

"Which war?" the man asked.

"All of them," Lucas said.

"Right on, brother." The man smiled, then turned his attention back to the stage.

There were four guys in the band; three black, one white, playing music like B. B. King's. But different, too, full of heart and juice. The walls were shaking. The whole audience was moving like one big multilimbed creature. I was moving too, because it feels so good when the music's right and you can hear how much the musicians love to do it. I understood Lucas better than I ever had before. Music moves through Lucas like currents through water. Water through water. Music through Lucas.

"What do you think?" he shouted in my ear.

"I like it!"

"What?"

"I like it!"

The band members recognized Lucas and asked him to sit in. As he strapped on the guitar, I went tight with fear. What if the crowd didn't like him? What if they turned away and left him naked onstage, Lucas stripped bare to the bone?

They loved him. They loved the place he took them. He played a liquid lead, the notes as clear as water; no show-off stuff, no ruffles, no extras, because you only need to do it right.

He was so good I forgot he was my brother.

I wondered what my parents would think if they could see him. It would probably make them sad and proud. Sad because Lucas was so into the music, he wasn't in this world anymore. And proud because he'd found someplace better.

When he finished the audience clapped and shouted, "All right! All right!" until Lucas couldn't help himself—he smiled.

Driving home, he even put on the heater. It smelled funny but it warmed my toes.

"Lucas." We were almost home.

"What?"

"You were fantastic."

He grunted but I knew he was pleased.

My father was waiting up for us, pretending he wasn't,

watching "The Tonight Show," which he hates.

"How was the concert?"

"Terrible," my brother said. "The man's sold out. But we went to this blues club—"

"Where?"

"In the city."

"Where in the city?"

"Down around Tenth."

"You took your sister to a black blues club?"

"No, Dad! I took her to the Black and Blue Club! It's an S and M bar! What do you think?"

"Can we all please stop shouting?" I said. "We had a wonderful time and now we're home safe. So everything's fine. We had a great time, Dad."

"But not at the concert," he sighed. My father never gives Lucas what he wants, no matter how hard he tries.

"That's not your fault," Lucas said. "The warm-up band was good."

I left them watching TV and went into the kitchen. Then we all drank tea and watched some red-haired comedian. She was screaming, "What a world we live in! Rush, rush, rush! If I died right now—which apparently I am!—it'd be a week before I had a chance to lie down! My schedule! I've got more irons in the fire than an arsonist at a golf club! But seriously!"

Dad conked out. Lucas and I kept sitting there. I didn't want the evening to end. And I didn't want to fall asleep.

"You should go to bed. You look tired," he said.

"I am."

"You still having those dreams?"

Lucas looked at me and I understood why all those girls like him. When you have his attention, it's one hundred percent. His eyes are like spotlights.

"Yeah," I said.

"Scary ones?"

I shook my head. I hate to talk about the dreams. It makes them real.

I said, "They're mostly about Helen."

Lucas nodded. "What's she doing in them?"

"Different things. Mostly dying," I said. "But not like in real life; more like a play. Last night she called me up and said she was going to come get me so we could go shopping. And I kept waiting, but she never got here. Bambi was in it, too."

"What a lucky break for you." Lucas thinks Bambi is an unintentional riot.

"She was telling me that Cheerios are doughnut seeds."

We laughed. My father snorted and rumbled on the sofa. "He's so cute when he's asleep," Lucas said.

The next thing I knew, he was jiggling me awake. He couldn't get Dad up, so he covered him with an afghan and turned off the TV set.

Lucas followed me up the stairs. I wanted to talk to him; to tell him how much I'd liked the music; how proud of him I am; how much I love him.

Instead, I said, "Thanks for taking me."

"It was fun." Lucas stopped outside his bedroom door and yawned. "Wake me up if the dreams get too weird. Or if you grow any doughnuts."

Then he went into his room.

## 5

FEBRUARY 15

*Geez, I used to write in here all the time, but lately I'm way behind. When you're not busy, you've got time to write in your journal and nothing to write about, and when lots of stuff is happening, you're too busy to write it down.*

*So, what's new:*

*I'm getting a story* (Blackbird) *published in the school literary magazine! This could be the start of something big! (Miss Modesty)*

*What else. Bambi's mother had her face lifted. She looks completely different. She looks like she can't close her eyes. Bambi thinks her mom looks terrific. She says when she's that age she's either going to kill herself or get her face lifted.*

*Personally, I think they lifted Mrs. Bordtz's face too far. She could pluck her eyebrows with her teeth.*

*Mom bought me a beautiful blue sweater the other day. Just for fun, she said, 'cause she thought I'd like it. I do!*

*Lucas has gotten a job in a music store, so he can make money during the day and go broke at night playing free gigs. Dad's not happy about the job. He wants Lucas to go back to college. He has this insane idea that Lucas is going through a phase, and that some morning he'll come down for breakfast in a suit and tie, freshly shaved. . . .*

*I got a C on my math test. Phooey. Or, as Sara Rose would say: Poopoo forever! She was so cute when I was over there the other night. I wonder if I'll have kids someday. That's kind of hard to picture, but I like them.*

*Bloomfield gave me a valentine.*

*I gave him one, of course, with this drippy poem I'd written, but I didn't think he'd have one for me. It's a little kid's valentine: "Bee mine, honey! You're sweet!" with a real nice note inside. He's different on paper than in person. Softer. He tells me what he couldn't say, i.e., that he likes the color of my hair; it looks warm.*

*The other night we had this big discussion about life, sitting in his car in front of the house. Jessie and the folks took turns peeking out the windows until he honked the horn and flashed the lights.*

*The moon was down and you could see a million stars. Bloomfield started talking about the universe (big subject) and how crazy it is to believe in God; life is just a freak accident and you might as well make the best of it, etc.*

*Then he asked did I believe in God, and I felt kind of*

*embarrassed telling him yes, since I can't explain it. I don't picture God as a guy in a white beard, or some game-show host awarding prizes ("Let's tell Helen what she's won!")*

*God is the feeling I have sometimes that we're, all of us in the world, connected; part of something large that we're too close to see, like those paintings made up of tiny dots that take shape only at a distance.*

*Of course, that all came out crazy, and I expected Bloomfield to argue. But he didn't.*

*He kissed me.*

*Bloomfield kissed me.*

*His lips were softer than I'd expected, smooth and warm and light. Then he pulled back and really looked into my eyes. Then he kissed me again and I kissed him back.*

*My stomach was all tight and fluttery.*

*His hand caressed my throat, then moved down my blouse. . . . I'd never let anyone touch me there before. His hands seemed made to fit me.*

*Mom would die if she read this.*

*I don't know what to think. I'm glad and scared—glad because I'd like to kiss him forever, and scared because I don't know what will happen. It seems like boys always try to sleep with you, then as soon as you do, they cross you off the list. (Attention, Mom! I'm not speaking from experience.) I've seen it happen to Bambi. She gets involved with all these guys, then never hears from them again. They pretend they don't know her. How can people be so cruel? And how can she be so stupid? She's so hungry for love, she pretends she's found it.*

*Sometimes I could shoot her parents. They've totally screwed her up. They can't be real with her for five seconds. Like, years ago, when she had to have her tonsils out, they told her she was going to a party. They dressed her up and curled her hair. The next thing she knows, she's being strapped to a gurney. . . .*

*Speaking of parties, Bloomfield and I went to Debbi's. Needless to say, her parents were away and the place was a madhouse: cars on the front lawn, the neighbors called the cops, etc. I got a headache from the noise and the cigarette smoke but I wasn't feeling that hot anyway. I'm having the damn chemotherapy again, every other week.*

*Bloomfield doesn't know about all that.*

*For one thing, there hasn't been much to say. Dr. Yee says things are basically under control and the chemo is just prevention. But I feel like hell when I have it. I stay home from school. Everybody thinks it's because of my periods or some kind of tricky hormonal deal. I'm afraid they'd act different if they knew the truth, start treating me like some fragile flower when I'd rather be a cactus, tough and prickly.*

*I feel guilty 'cause I haven't told Bloomfield the truth. We're supposedly having a relationship (or something) and trying to be honest with each other. But I'm scared if I told him it would blow his mind. He doesn't like things to get too heavy.*

*Of course, I'll have to tell him eventually, especially if I go bald. (My hair, Bloomfield? Oh, didn't I mention it? I decided to shave my head.) I haven't lost much yet but there's a lot in my brush, and what's left feels like sofa stuffing. Dr. Yee says it might not be a big problem; we'll have to wait and see (I love surprises!); but in the meantime I might consider getting a wig.*

That's out. Some of the kids at the clinic wear wigs and it's so obvious, they might as well have arrows pointing to their heads. Mom says we could find a good one, but I'd still feel like Dolly Parton.

If it keeps falling out, I'll have to do something. I picture Bloomfield and me at Foothill Park, lying in the cool grass, kissing. Then we rise, and as we walk off into the sunset together, he points to the ground and says, Wait, you forgot your hair.

I can't stand this.

At least my face isn't puffed up (yet), so that's something.

They've got me in group counseling at the clinic, mostly with people my age. Compared to some of them, I'm in really good shape, which makes me feel better and worse, simultaneously. (Whenever Jessie hears the expression "Things could be worse," she says, "They will be." You'd think she and Bloomfield would get along, but they don't.)

I like the group therapist. She's young and snappy. She has us doing visualization: Imagine your healthy blood cells conquering the bad ones. Picture Chemo gobbling up a cancer mouse.

Last week we did this really neat thing. She put on some beautiful guitar music and told us to close our eyes. We were going to take a train trip in our minds. It could be any type of train we chose, brand new and streamlined or a locomotive.

It was a long, smooth ride. Nancy, the therapist, described the countryside, rolling hills and snow-frosted mountains, pastures purple with lupine.

At last we stopped by a brilliant blue lake. Can you see it?

*Nancy said. Now you're diving in. The water is cool. You're diving deep to find a treasure chest. Deeper and deeper. You see it shining on the lake floor. Swimming is as effortless as breathing.*

*There, you have it. Lift it up. It's easy. You're swimming toward the surface, toward the sky.*

*Now you're back on land. Open your chests, she said, and see what kind of treasure you find.*

*One girl found diamonds, rubies, emeralds. One boy found a book he'd written. Another boy found a silver key. One girl found a smiling baby girl. That kid who always wears the baseball cap found a letter, but he wouldn't say what was in it. He cried.*

*I had a hard time describing the treasure I was seeing. It crowded all the words from my mind. It was light, golden, glowing light, radiating warmth, growing brighter and brighter.*

*Is it scary? asked the therapist, and I said no. The light was coming from me.*

*Then we all took our treasures and got back on our trains and rode home again and opened our eyes.*

## 6

I WAS SITTING ON THE BENCH OUTSIDE THE EMPORIUM, WAIT-ing for Bambi, who is always late.

On her tombstone it will say: The Late Bambi Sue Bordtz.

Someone honked their car horn but I didn't look.

Next, the honker whistled, then shouted, "Hey, blondie!"

If I turned my head every time someone whistled, I'd have to wear a neck brace.

I looked when the honker shouted, "Hey, Monkeyface!"

I knew that voice. Bloomfield was parked by the curb, leaning out his car window with that curdled smile Helen found so irresistible.

"What do you want?" I said.

"It was great talking to you the other night," Bloomfield said. "Really boosted my ego."

"Too bad you hung up. I was just getting started."

He looked away, then back at me again. "What's your problem?" he demanded.

"You know."

"If I knew, I wouldn't ask."

"I'm not going to sit here and shout at you!" I shouted.

"Then come over to the car so we can talk."

"My mother told me to never talk to strangers, and you're as strange as they get."

"Hey, listen!" Bloomfield sneered, redfaced.

"No, you listen! Just because you feel like a guilty creep, don't expect me to make you feel better! Or to tell you everything's fine when it's not!"

"I don't know what the hell you're talking about!"

"Hi, Bloomfield." Bambi materialized beside me, in a tiny T-shirt, aiming her braless breasts at Bloomfield's car.

He ignored her. "Listen, Jess, I don't know what your problem is, but don't take it out on me, okay? I called you up the other night because I thought we could be friends."

"After what you did?"

"What did I do?"

"Forget it! Just forget it!"

"All right! I give up!" He smashed the car door with his fist and pulled into the traffic.

"He seems upset," Bambi said. "Don't you know how to flirt?"

I stalked inside the crowded mall. It's huge and new and the stores are so ritzy, people dress up to go shopping.

"You're making a big mistake," Bambi said. "Bloomfield's pretty cute."

"Don't you ever think about anything but boys?"

"Like what? Oh, wait a minute, Jess. I'm going to get a beauty make-over."

Bambi slid onto a stool at the Macy's cosmetics counter, where a woman with pink hair waited to transform her.

"You know what your problem is, Jess?" she said, while the woman drew blue moons around her eyes.

"Yeah, I know what my problem is."

"Your problem is, you're way too critical of guys. You'll always be alone if you don't lighten up. You know what my mother says?"

"Tell me. I must know." I splashed myself with sample perfumes.

"She says all men are dogs."

"She's right," the makeup artist said, ladling on mascara. Bambi's eyes looked like the scene of a tragic forest fire.

"That's what she says. She says all men are dogs."

"Does she say that about your father, too?" The Bordtzes have been talking divorce since Bambi was born; stuck with each other like an ugly pair of shoes, no good together, no good apart.

"Well, sure," Bambi said. "He's a perfect example. He completely takes her for granted, like she's always been there and always will be. Which is true. Who'd marry her?"

"He did."

"Yeah, when she was young and pretty. Now she's old."

"How old is old?" asked the makeup artist, painting Bambi's mouth a frigid purple.

"I don't know," Bambi said. "Thirty-eight, I think."

The woman groaned.

"No, wait. She's forty. Or forty-one."

The woman gouged Bambi's face with blusher, futilely trying to sculpt hollows in cheeks like candy apples.

"Anyway," Bambi said, "you should go out with Bloomfield. He's very good-looking."

"So? He dumped my sister." Mingled perfumes filled my nose. I had to grab the counter. I felt dizzy. "He dumped her because you told him she had cancer."

"I didn't mean to," Bambi whined, fidgeting. The makeup artist wandered off to sharpen an eyebrow pencil. Say the word cancer and everyone splits. Which is ridiculous, because it isn't always fatal.

Did the cancer kill Helen, or was it the cure—all that poison flooding her veins?

"He would've found out anyway," Bambi insisted. "She was wearing a wig."

Helen and I picked it out together, trying to make a joke of it, shopping in places with names like Wig World.

"Where's Vincent Price?" Helen had whispered when we walked into the House of Hair. The room was full of foam mannequin heads draped with all kinds of wigs; some as obvious as hats, some as subtle as if they'd been snipped off sleeping children.

"Those are real hair," the saleswoman told us proudly. We were afraid to ask her whose.

Helen tried on a bunch of wigs. Some of them cracked us up. Helen as a movie star. Helen as president of the P.T.A. The one she bought was long and brown and thick, just like her own hair before it changed.

"Oh boy," Helen said, gazing at it in the mirror. "Mom will never have to cut my bangs again."

She'd been so nervous about wearing it to school, afraid it would fall off. It didn't; it fit so snugly she was glad to take it off at night. At home she just wore a bandanna. That bandanna made my brother and dad so nervous they couldn't look her in the eyes.

"It was a good wig," I told Bambi. "It wasn't all the same color." Good wigs are shaded, like heads of real hair. "Anyway, it was none of your business."

"I didn't mean to tell him!" Bambi sniveled. "We were talking and it slipped out. I thought he knew!"

"Well, he didn't. And as soon as he did, he took off."

That bastard Bloomfield will burn in hell for betraying my sister. When he ran into her at school, he looked away.

I would wake up in the night and hear Helen crying, but I didn't know what to say.

"All done!" announced the makeup artist. "What do you think?"

"I love it!" Bambi beamed at the mirror. She's gotten the idea that she can be a fashion model. She takes classes at Mannequin Magic. They're teaching her to walk down a runway. If she can't be a model, she can strip.

"What do you think, Jess? Could I be in the movies?"

"Absolutely." We're talking Betty Boop, not Betty Bacall.

It's hard to be chic in the Chubette department. Bambi bought a bunch of clothes without trying them on. When she gets home she'll throw them on her bedroom floor, as if layers of sweaters and blouses and dresses could keep out the cold.

I couldn't find a thing I wanted. It all looked tacky and cheap. Nowadays you pay big bucks for clothes that are prefaded.

I started feeling fuzzy and remembered that I hadn't eaten breakfast that morning or dinner the night before. Food has become a problem. It doesn't interest me. The smell of it leaves me weak.

"All you need is a taco," Bambi said. So we went to the mall's upper floor, where the food concessions are located. Bambi ordered a jumbo Tiki taco, a double order of fries, and a root-beer float. I picked at a plate of cold nachos.

"Gawd," Bambi groaned. "I'm so sick of this diet. I wish I was naturally skinny like you."

"It's easy," I said. "You just quit eating." When Helen's pants were so big they fell off, she said *What a way to get down to a size eight.* . . .

"Hey, isn't that?—No, never mind," Bambi sighed. "I thought that guy was Ted."

One of the many frogs in Bambi's quest for the prince.

They'd met on the phone; wrong number. After weeks of ridiculous, sleazy conversations, they'd decided to meet, at the mall. I went with her to absorb some of the shock. He wasn't tall and handsome; he was short and squat. And he had the nerve to say to Bambi, "You didn't sound fat on the phone."

It took hours to talk her out of killing herself. She thinks if she did that, people would finally take her seriously.

No, you're not fat, I'd said, you're comfortable, you're cozy. Besides, thin's not in anymore. Who has all the boyfriends: me or you?

"Forget about Ted," I said now. "He was a phony."

"I'd like to meet somebody real, for a change," she agreed, tapping her fake fingernails on the greasy tabletop. The nails are so long that she's handicapped. She bites her real ones down to the nub.

"Forget about boys for a while," I said. "You know what your mom says. Bow wow."

"She should talk," Bambi scoffed. "I wouldn't have picked my father if he was the last one on the rack."

The nachos I'd eaten were suddenly coming back up. I clamped my teeth shut to keep them in. The roar of all the talking, laughing people overwhelmed me. I had to leave. I had to leave.

"What's the matter, Jess?"

There wasn't time to explain. I had to get out of the mall. The walls and roof and people squeezed me, threading into my ears like steel.

"Jessie!" Bambi's round, worried face goggled at me. We were outside; I was sitting on a cool stone bench. My breath was coming in gasps and chunks.

"Nothing's wrong," I finally managed. "I was starting to feel funny. It must've been all those perfumes I sampled."

"You scared me half to death!" Bambi pouted. "Now can we go get an ice-cream cone?"

We didn't get an ice-cream cone. I made her take me home. The windows were open but I was sweating. The ride was an obstacle course. Cars unexpectedly cut into our lane, bicyclists popped up by the front bumper, pedestrians threatened to somersault across the hood.

I was sure we were going to be killed any second.

Bambi dropped me off. "I'll call you later," she promised. I ran up the walk, up the stairs, into my room. It was a good half hour before my heart stopped pounding.

This wasn't the first time this had happened, but the worst. A few days before, Lucas had taken me to a movie, and I'd started fritzing out while we were waiting in line.

"I have to go," I told him.

"There's a bathroom inside."

"I mean home."

"What?" Lucas groaned. "Don't tell me you're having another attack. We've been waiting in line for an hour."

I made him leave. He dumped me off, then split. When Mom asked what was wrong, I told her cramps.

I don't know what to make of this development. This sort of thing never used to happen. Since Helen died, I've been experiencing . . . technical difficulties. Please stand by. No adjustment of your set is necessary.

Any second the picture is supposed to come back.

But it doesn't. Nothing comes back.


When I fall asleep that night, I dream I'm driving. I'm driving Lucas's Impala. The ocean's on my right, shining like steel, almost blinding me.

There's not much traffic. None at all, in fact, which is odd. It's such a perfect day you'd think the traffic would be thick.

There's a hitchhiker up ahead. He doesn't get closer, no matter how far or how fast I drive. The speedometer inches up; I'm doing sixty, seventy; whipping around curves that are sheer cliffs.

Now the hitchhiker's close. It's a man. A dog. A man; I know this although he has no face, just white eyes in a dark hood. He runs into the road in front of the Impala— My God! He's on the hood of the car, that faceless face pressed against the windshield, his empty eyes only inches from mine.

I floor the gas pedal. He loses his grip; his fingers streak the glass as he rolls onto the roof. Then he crashes off, bouncing down the cliffs, hundreds of feet— God, I didn't mean to kill him!

But when I turn the corner he's dead ahead, eyes burning, his thumb stretched out.

## 7

MARCH 13

*I'm sitting for the Harrises tonight. It's late. I just tiptoed in to check the boys and Sara. Her mouth looked like a piece of pink candy. So sweet! She comes over to the house and calls: "Hel-le-en! Hel-le-en! Can you come out and play?"*

*Sara Rose is my favorite favorite.*

*Thought I'd bring this with me and try to catch up. As usual, I'm way behind. Life in the fast lane (in a slow car). When did life get so speeded up? I'm tired. I'm tired of being so tired. I look like death on a dinner roll lately.*

*Enough complaining.*

*We seem to be embarked on a family campaign to achieve Normalcy In Our Lifetime. It's exhausting, not to mention impossible. We don't seem normal but then, who is? The polished people in the TV sitcoms? Bloomfield's Popsicle parents? Bambi's folks, Mr. and Mrs. Godzilla?*

*It's comical. We're Going Places Together all the time now: Mom and Dad arguing about which route to take; Lucas in the backseat, rolling his eyes; Jessie by the other window, in case she has to puke or jump out. (She's so WEIRD lately, so uptight, as if she could burst into tears any second. Jessie never cries.)*

*Then there's me, in the middle, like peanut butter, sticking everything together.*

*Poor Helen.*

*They never say that, but I know that's what they're thinking.*

*I'll tell you something: I'm not going to die. I'm going to stay alive to see a million mornings, and play with Sara Rose, and write some really good stories, so good that other writers like them, not just my family.*

*I want to make love and get married (maybe). I want to have a baby or two. I can't imagine not having a child. I mean, they're a pain in the behind sometimes, but they see things fresh and new. Tonight Sara Rose said, "The stars are like night lights." She told me I'm her favorite cook. What about your mom? I asked. "She's my favorite, too."*

*The thing is, I have to keep fighting the cancer. Sometimes I'm afraid that if I fall asleep, I won't wake up; I'll sleep forever. But if I don't get enough rest, I won't be strong enough to handle the chemo. It's murder. The therapist says, Visualize your healthy cells as brave knights on spangled horses, striking down the bad cells, conquering the cancer, on the red field of battle. My bloodstream.*

*Sometimes it's like watching a movie: What will our heroine do next? How will she save herself?*

*Then I remember: This is real. This is me. Why is this happening?*

*I'm rambling. I was talking about THE FAMILY.*

*THE FAMILY! In all their heartbreaking glory. I love them so much. They drive me crazy. We're all such characters, playing ourselves, locked into our stubborn roles. I wouldn't have Dad's; it's too demanding. He's always working. I guess he likes it. I hope so. There seems to be a lot of anxiety connected to the office, not to the work itself, but to the back-stabbing and buck-passing; the politics. Some people will do anything to get ahead, Dad says. He doesn't step on anyone's toes, which takes some fancy footwork. If only he would be more diplomatic with Lucas. But Lucas is just as bad.*

*Dad: In the coming years—*

*Lucas: Which years? They're all coming.*

*Lucas is such a grouch these days. He's trying to start a band and grow a mustache simultaneously, which apparently is a tremendous strain. I shouldn't tease him but I can't help it; I love to see him play his part. His face grows red, his eyebrows whiten. . . . He looks pretty handsome when he's not geeking out, and he's the best guitarist I've ever heard. I'm not saying that because he's my brother. It's true. At Christmastime he played a carol for me, an instrumental version of "Joy to the World." Acoustically, not electrically. It was so holy it made me cry.*

*Sometimes he sings songs I think he makes up. About love and longing and loneliness. I wonder if Lucas has ever made love. I wish we could talk about that kind of stuff. That would be* helpful for me, in regard to Bloomfield, who is on my mind all the time.

I was talking about the family. I keep wandering away from them, like Lucas does whenever the five of us are out in public together. He stands at a distance, a store detective, keeping an eye on the escaped criminals. Or he acts like it's spring break at the institution; the lunatics are out for the day and he's our attendant.

I just remembered the time a million years ago when we were on our way to the beach, and Lucas wrote that sign and held it up in the back of the car: HELP! I'VE BEEN KIDNAPPED. A squadron of Highway Patrol cars flagged us down; guns were pointed at Dad's head.

He was just kidding, Lucas said.

He's not crazy. But he's in between normal and nuts. The same with Dad. They're so intense! Those guys are like the tide; the arguments keep coming but the beach is still there, no matter how many waves crash on it, and it always will be, as long as there's a sea.

The main difference between them is thirty years.

Today we had lunch at Wally's Harbor House, overlooking the bay. We made it through the meal without an argument (a miracle!), but Lucas and Dad started as soon as we got back in the car.

Dad said synthesizers serve a musical purpose and just because they're not instruments per se is no reason to write them off.

Lucas said Dad thinks everything new is good, simply because it's new, and the bigger the better. Synthesizers are machines, Lucas said. He cranked up the radio. Can you tell me what kind *of instrument that is? Flute, strings, guitar? Sounds a little bit like everything and a lot like nothing. That's a synthesizer, Lucas said. Just plug it in and it plays itself. No need to hang around making music.*

*In a normal family the father would push the traditional stuff while the son led a revolution into the future. Not the Castles. Lucas is on a one-man crusade to bring back the past.*

*I imagine seeing him on the evening news, arrested for blowing up the Institute for the Study of Advanced Technology. His parents claim, "He's always been spunky."*

*Lucas is a human cowlick.*

*Why must he argue with Dad all the time? He's never going to change him; Dad's been Dad for fifty years. Lucas should let things ride sometimes. He jumps on everything Dad says. THE COMING YEARS? EXACTLY WHICH YEARS DO YOU MEAN, MR. CASTLE? AREN'T THEY ALL COMING? ISN'T THAT, IN FACT, HOW YOU WOULD DESCRIBE THE FUTURE? I REST MY CASE!*

*We all played Monopoly the other night. It was like some kind of boring torture. Mom fell asleep in the middle of the game while Lucas was giving a speech about the importance of the peace movement in ending the Vietnam War.*

*Lucas had a fit.*

*Mom woke with a snort. "I was picturing what you were saying in my mind," she insisted. If I were her, I'd tell Lucas to shut up, but she always apologizes.*

*Bambi is getting on my nerves lately. You'd think I'd be used* to her by now. Feeling sorry for someone isn't the same thing as liking them. It doesn't matter if I like her; I love her. I have to. But MUST she make every sentence a question? "So we go to the show, you know? And these guys? They're over by the snackbar? In black leather, you know? And they ask me my name?"

When someone asks her name, she answers: Bambi Sue Bordtz? As if she isn't sure. Bambi Sue Who?

She's going out with this meathead jerk. When he can't think of anything to say (most of the time), he picks her up and holds her over his head.

On the other hand, silence CAN be golden. "That wig looks really real," Bambi told me. Me: "So how did you know it was a wig?" Her: "You can tell."

I'm so glad I don't have to wear it yet. I was afraid it would fall off during p.e., but I don't have to take p.e. anymore. Everybody thinks it has something to do with my period. I'm famous for my legendary cramps.

Something funny happened at dinner the other night. It was Lucas's birthday, and Aunt Linda, who thinks we're all still in grade school, sent him a present: a little cloth animal of unknown species, its back slit open, spewing Kleenex.

Lucas figured the present was inside, so he pulled out all the Kleenex. It turned out the present was the Kleenex and the animal's a handy dispenser.

It's amazing that Lucas is so old. Twenty. After the family party (we gave him music stuff and some shirts he'll never wear), he went out with friends and didn't come home until the next day. Mom and Dad stayed up till 1 a.m., arguing. Dad wanted to wait up for Lucas. Mom said Lucas was a grown man now, believe it or not, and they had to trust him.

I wonder if I can trust Bloomfield.

Would he go away if he knew about the cancer?

When I kiss him I worry that my breath smells funny. Do I taste like medicine? Apparently not: We kiss until my lips are puffy (mostly at his house; his parents work), and he runs his hands up and down my back, then squeezes my breasts and whispers, "Helen, why not?"

Trouble is, I can't think of a good reason. Besides death and disease and babies, of course.

I love him and I want to touch him and I want him to touch me.

The other night I dreamed we were at Foothill Park, in that flower-sprinkled meadow. Bloomfield was wearing a white tuxedo (!) and playing a piano, just grandly. I was dancing, leaping, soaring, iridescent as dragonfly wings. . . .

I'd lose my breath if I danced like that now. That's the lovely thing about dreams. You can be so free.

There's too much going on all the time: school & family & clinic & writing. I want to write something perfect for Bloomfield, a story that would knock his socks off, a poem that would kiss his heart.

I know that the way I feel about him is crazy. I really don't know him at all. But for some strange reason he makes me happy. When I'm with him I am laughing, dancing, flying.

O Bloomfield: I love/I'm so scared of you. I wish I had the guts to say: It may be true that life's in vain, but I would do it all again with you.

## 8

BAMBI AND I CUT CLASS TODAY. WE DIDN'T EVEN DISCUSS IT. When she picked me up this morning I tossed my books into the backseat, hard. She looked at me and laughed, then we just cruised.

I know I should buckle down and study but it's hard to take the future seriously. At any second the earth could veer off course and slam into the sun. Or a meteorite could land on your head. Twelve tons of them fall every day.

I was never the great brain, compared to Helen.

I can't seem to concentrate.

We drove to San Jose and toured the Winchester Mystery House. It's a giant pipe dream of a mansion, built by an old lady with tons of dough. Her husband invented the Winchester rifle, which killed thousands of people, who haunted his widow. She believed that as long as she kept building—rooms, turrets, porches, stairways—she would never die. She was wrong.

After that we had burgers and milkshakes. The waitress eyed us suspiciously. Bambi was done up in her junior hooker outfit: black fishnet stockings and a slinky dress that hugged her like an oil slick. Gulping down the last bite of her wolfburger, she said: "I feel so fat! I must be getting my period."

I hope so. Last month she slept with a thirty-year-old guy because she thought it would be rude to tell him no.

She sets traps for herself, promptly falls into them, and then shrieks, "Who turned out the lights?"

Nobody, you idiot. Open your eyes.

It sure is easy to see other people's problems, but not your own.

There was nothing to do. That's the trouble with cutting; all your friends are at school.

When in doubt, shop. I didn't have any money, but Bambi had her magic plastic cards.

It was November in the parking lot and December in the mall. It's been decorated for Christmas since Labor Day. We went to the Emporium. We went to Macy's. Bambi bought purple vinyl boots, designer jeans, and perfume. Helen had to give up wearing perfume. The chemo made her skin smell funny.

I only bought a lipstick. I was feeling nervous. I was thinking about my teachers. They were real nice to me after Helen died, but now it's business as usual. They're ticked because I have so much "untapped potential." I'm not doing my homework, or forget to bring it, and I never raise my hand in class. Helen and I were secretly shy. Together, we made someone brave.

We drove back to Bambi's down streets alive with cartwheeling leaves, the tape deck blasting, the top down although the day was cool. Bambi hates silence and she loves to be looked at. It's the only time she's sure she's alive.

She lives a few blocks from me in a ritzy development named for what used to be there: Buckhorn Hill. Everybody calls it Big Bucksville.

Her grandfather founded Bordtz Beer and made a killing during Prohibition. Bordtz Beer eventually went down the toilet, but Bambi's dad held onto his inheritance and invested in real estate. He owns several tasty chunks of the town.

Their house is huge. It's got an indoor pool, a sauna, and a hot tub, all unused. Bambi's mother was watching the tube in the den. She prefers TV to real life. Mrs. Bordtz is as spooky as a sleepwalker, with eyes like keyholes to burning rooms. She's always dressed up, even when she's going nowhere, as if waiting for the press to arrive.

"Is that you, Bambi?" she called.

"No, it's a blood-crazed maniac. We're going to slaughter you and torch the house."

"Oh, is Jessie there, too? Shouldn't you girls be in school?"

"It's a holiday, Ma. Sid Vicious's birthday."

"Oh. There's fresh Twinkies in the fridge."

We ate some Twinkies in the gleaming kitchen. Twice a week a Spanish woman comes in and shovels out the dirt. I forget her name. She doesn't speak English. She doesn't speak to us at all.

Bambi's mother floated in and watched us eat. Her hair was newly shorn; but not as if she'd had it styled; as if she'd gone berserk with the scissors.

"How are you, Jessie?" Her voice was very flat. She always talks like that, no matter what she's saying.

"Fine."

"That's good."

Bambi poured some 7-Up. It galloped into the glasses.

"Where's Rascal?" I asked. Their obnoxious beagle. He's usually humping my leg.

"Gone," Mrs. Bordtz said vaguely.

"We got rid of him when we got the new furniture," Bambi explained. "Want to see it? It's Mediterranean."

After I dutifully admired the furniture warehouse that passes for a home, we retreated to Bambi's bedroom. She shoved stuff off the bed so we could sit down, then proceeded to paint her toenails green while talking nonstop about this jerk she's seeing. He wants her to tattoo his name on her breast. He prefers black hair, so she's dyeing it again. She's getting more holes punched in her ears.

I will never cut my hair. I will let it grow forever and wear it like a cloak, like a cape. Helen had the longest, thickest, prettiest hair before it changed.

Bambi thumbed through the *Star*. "Wow, they've taught plants to read! Hey, look at this kid's nose! He looks like an anteater!"

"I have to go now, Bambi."

"Why?" She looked startled. She never wants me to leave.

"Mom will be expecting me."

Besides, I couldn't breathe. There's no air in that house. It smells like the clinic that Helen went to; like flesh, like fading flowers.

My mother was making dinner.

"How was school, honey?"

"Fine." She has enough on her mind.

"Bloomfield called again."

"Big wow," I said.

"He seems like a very nice boy."

"Looks can be deceiving."

"You should call him back."

I wanted to escape but she wanted to talk. Mom used to talk to Helen. Helen would've looked like this in twenty years: smooth brown hair, a slender figure. I noticed she was more than slender. When had she grown so thin? A glass of red wine was on the counter. My mother used to drink only at parties and celebrations.

To my surprise, I launched into a rollicking fabrication of my hilarious day at school, making up all this jazz about a football rally, and the joke my sociology teacher told the class: "Marriage is a lot like the gallows. After a while you get the hang of it." Ha.

My mother smiled, her bleak eyes brightening. Her smile was a drug. I went on and on, like some crazed talk-show host, like that red-haired comedian. *People! You hear about the optimistic drunk who fell out of a high-rise bar? At each floor she shouted to the folks inside: "Doing all right so far!"*

I thought to myself: I am a fabulous liar. I should be a writer. I should be a politician.

It made my mother happy; that was all that mattered. So what if none of it was true? For a few minutes she forgot that her life had been shattered; that she would never again see the daughter who wore her face; forgot her broken-hearted husband, stranded in a sand trap, beating golf balls to death; forgot the angry alien masquerading as her son, who plays his guitar just as loud as he can, to fill his mind with music, to drive out the pain; forgot the tangle-haired tightrope walker who is losing her balance.

"I ran into Mrs. Maxson today," Mom said. "She used to work at the library, remember? She hadn't heard about Helen."

"What did you tell her?"

My mother's eyes probed my face. "I told her she'd died."

The last time that happened to me, I lied. I said, "Helen's gone away to school."

Death is hard, Dr. Shubert says, but life is even harder. Jessie, she says, you must face the truth.

I said, "I'm going upstairs."

My mother's face collapsed, her happiness a crumpled mask. I had not fooled her.

"It's bad enough we've lost Helen!" she cried. "Now we're losing you!"

She ran from the room. I should've gone after her. Instead, I went up and fell asleep on my bed, curled around Helen's journal.

I open my eyes. Pitch blackness. Where am I? In my room, in my bed, in the middle of the night. My bed is a boat in a dark sea.

Why did I wake? The smell. It's smoke.

Fire! The bedroom door is outlined in orange neon.

I get out of bed and touch the door. It's hot; it burns my fingers. In sixth grade the fire chief talked to our class. He said, "Jessie, don't open that door."

I run to the window. I can't get it open. It's stuck where Lucas painted it. I've got to get out. I can hear the hungry flames devouring the living room, licking up the stairs.

I pick up my school books and smash the window. The glass shrieks and chatters. I climb out.

Neighbors line the lawn, in robes and pajamas. They see me and gasp. "Jump, Jessie!" they shout. "You have to jump! You have no choice!"

I'm falling through space. I land in a shrub. Thorns rip my skin. Someone's pulling me out. It's Bambi's mother, her eyes full of the flames, the red light flickering on her face.

"Look at all the people," she says, calmly, as if she were announcing the time. "Two A.M.," she adds, reading my mind.

The crowd is enormous. A man sells hot dogs. "Red hots!" he shouts. "Red hots!"

Dad is beside me. He takes my arm. "Come on, honey," he says. "Everybody's waiting."

The Ford's parked in the street, Mom up front, Lucas in the backseat, his face turned away from me.

"Where are we going, Daddy?" I ask.

"To our new house. You'll like it, Jessie."

"But all our stuff—"

"We'll buy new stuff." He opens the car door. "Get in, honey."

I slide in beside Lucas. Then I remember.

"Helen's in the house!"

I can't open my door. Very gently Dad says, "It's too late."

"Helen's in there!" I'm screaming. "We've got to save her!"

But we don't. We drive away. I look out the back window. The house is blazing. Tongues of flame stick out the windows, flames as orange-blue as veins. The walls shudder, then collapse.

I am screaming Helen's name.

My eyes snap open. Pitch blackness. Where am I? In my room, in my bed, in the middle of the night. The clock glows like a jack-o'-lantern. Two A.M.

Helen's bed is empty. My father was right.

## 9

MARCH 23

*Bloomfield and I drove to the ocean today—after an hour of instructions from Dad: Drive slowly, wear your seat belts, don't pick up hitchhikers, etc. I wouldn't have been a bit surprised if he'd tailed us in an unmarked car.*

*Bloomfield was wearing his jeans jacket and looked ultracool in blue.*

*It was the first time we'd ever gone out of town together and I felt like— It's a good thing nobody can read my mind. I was pretending we were married.*

*Oh, I have gotten so sappy lately! I want to touch him and hug him all the time! The other day he said, "Why are you smiling?" "No reason," I said. "I'm just happy."*

*The car ride made me a little nauseous. For a few dangerous seconds, I thought I was going to puke. Then I told myself: Will you please calm down? And miraculously, I did.*

*It was BEAUTIFUL at the beach! Clear and breezy, not too cold, and not many people around. We unpacked our stuff between two big rocks that shielded us from the wind.*

*We'd brought chicken and French bread and apples and cheese. Bloomfield ate like the world was on fire. He's always in a hurry; like, if he doesn't grab fun fast, someone might snatch it away. I guess that's what happens when you have a lot of brothers. Bloomfield is the runt of the litter.*

*After we ate I felt a little urpy, but the feeling passed in a while.*

*We walked along the shore and looked for bottle glass and shells. Bottle glass is my favorite; it's jagged edges smoothed soft by the waves, smoky-colored and mysterious.*

*Bloomfield talked and I listened. If Jessie read that, she'd say, He's such a chauvinist! But he's not; he hardly ever talks. When he does, it's precious as a soap bubble. The moment is that fragile.*

*Besides, there's so much I can't talk to him about. Bloomfield's body is hard and strong. He has no patience with patients. He suggested we climb some cliffs, but I pleaded fear of heights. My legs have become undependable.*

*Later (here it comes, Ma) we lay down on the blanket and looked into each other's eyes. Or tried to; he had on mirror sunglasses.*

*Him: "What's the matter?"*

*Me: "Nothing."*

*Him: "You look kind of strange."*

*Me: "I'm staring at myself."*

*Him: "You mean my glasses?"*

*He took them off. His eyes looked like chips of the sea.*

*He said, "I like you, Helen."*

*Me: "I like you, too."*

*Him: "You're not like most girls. You're—I don't know."*

*He kissed me, deeply, sweet and warm. A current was carrying me. We floated away, our arms around each other.*

*Bloomfield was on top of me.*

*I freaked out. I got scared. He said: "Don't worry; I brought a rubber."*

*I said: "That's not it."*

*"Is it the place? Is it too public? We can go back to my house."*

*"No," I said.*

*"Don't you want to?"*

*"I do," I said. "But I'm just not ready."*

*Bloomfield looked into my eyes as if he was reading my mind. "Are you a virgin?" he asked, and when I said yes, he got this look on his face that I couldn't name. He sat up and took my hand and said, "Let's walk."*

*We walked along the shore, the wind in our faces, and I finally asked him, "Are you mad?"*

*He stopped and held me, his breath warm on my cheek. He said, "I don't ever want to hurt you, Helen. You're so special."*

*"How?" I asked, wanting him to shower me with compliments, but he just kissed me.*

*We sat beside a tide pool, holding hands. I pressed my lips to his starfish palm. I wished that we could stay there forever, in a driftwood house with bottle glass windows spilling jewels of light on the polished stone floor. We would fall asleep cradled* on the breast of the ocean, knowing that our love, like the breath of the tide, would live on and on.

Instead, we went back to my house and listened to Lucas and Dad argue. Lucas can be such a mutant. Then Dad said something about Cretins Clearwater. . . . They're shouting at each other through a thick glass wall. They see the lips move but they don't hear the words.

Mom asked Bloomfield to stay for dinner. It was excruciating. Dad and Lucas stared at Bloomfield like he was an escaped lunatic. Mom filled the awkward conversational gaps with fascinating facts about my childhood. Meanwhile, Jessie rolled her eyes like a wild horse every time Bloomfield made a joke. She's such a twit lately; always moping around. If I don't do what she wants, she throws a fit. (She wanted me to take her shopping today. Why won't she get her driver's permit?!?)

It's not that I don't want to be close to Jess—we just need some breathing room. A lot of people like her but she won't make friends; she keeps to herself or ends up hanging out with Bambi, who drives her crazy. It seems like Jessie is jealous of Bloomfield, but when I said that, she blew a fuse.

On the school front: I LOVE my creative writing class. Ms. Tormey is an inspiration. She says I have the talent to make it big, but that perseverance is just as important; that I must develop a thick skin to endure criticism and rejection. (The thick skin I've got; I thought that nurse would never find a vein the other day! What's a little rejection when you're used to being stabbed?)

Sometimes I worry that there won't be enough time; that I'll die before I have a chance to get famous. But it's not really fame *that I want. (Sure.) I want to be a good writer. I want to capture life on paper.*

*Then I think: Who knows how long their ride will last? You live to old age if you're lucky, and duck the accidents and madmen and floods. . . . In a world this nuts, it's amazing so many children live to be adults.*

*In other words, I try not to worry.*

*I've been working on a short story that stinks and a poem that I like pretty well. And I've started making notes for this book I have in mind. I'll call it* How to Survive Your Life, *and it will be full of odds and ends and helpful hints, like: If you don't want people to know you've been crying, apply Preparation H to swollen eyelids. Works like a charm but it makes you squint. Thanks to Bambi Sue Bordtz for this beauty tip!*

*And I'll include recipes for success, like this one Mrs. Thompson taught us in Home Ec:*

Cinnamon Toast

| Bread | Cinnamon |
| Butter or Margarine | Sugar |

Carefully Toast Bread. Melt One Cube Of Butter Over Low Heat On Top Of Stove. Add One Teaspoon Cinnamon And One Tablespoon Sugar. Stir Continually, Being Careful Not to Burn. Use Basting Brush To—

*Jeez! someone shouted. Make a production out of it! Why not just sprinkle cinnamon and sugar on toast? Mrs. Thompson threw her out.*

*The book would contain words that people need to know. Like: Catkin. I love that word. Fuzzy buds on bare branches. Catkin is the name I'll call my daughter.*

*And it would offer cheap advice (a penny for my thoughts) like: In the game of tag with Time, you're always it.*

*The other night I dreamed I was in surgery, and this doctor I'd never seen before (where was Dr. Yee?) was cutting off my arm, then a leg, etc., examining them, and saying: "This one looks fine." I tried to protest but I couldn't speak. A phone kept ringing and ringing. The doctor finally answered and held it out to me. I was afraid it was God, but it was Bambi.*

MY MOTHER TAPPED ON MY BEDROOM DOOR AND SAID, "JESSIE, there's someone here to see you."

"If it's Bambi, tell her I joined the Peace Corps."

My mother didn't answer. Her footsteps faded down the hall.

I drew back the curtains and looked out my bedroom windows, down to the front door below. Nobody was there. Only Bloomfield.

In a few minutes my mother came back. "Didn't you hear me?" she called through the locked door. "You've got company."

"Tell him to go away," I said.

"I'll do no such thing. You open this door." She rattled the knob until I obeyed. "Now, you listen to me," she said when we were face to face. "I don't know what's come over you, Jessie, but I will not tolerate rudeness. You spend all your time locked up in this room—"

"I don't feel good. Maybe I'm getting the flu."

"You're not getting the flu," my mother said. "Dr. Shubert says—"

"She's been blabbing to you? So much for confidentiality."

"Jessie." Mom raised her hand and I flinched. That flinch caused her so much pain. "I wasn't going to hit you!" She cupped my chin. "Jessie," she crooned, searching my eyes with her own, "what am I going to do with you? Dr. Shubert says you can't accept the fact that Helen's dead."

"Of course I don't," I snapped. "Do you?"

My mother shrugged helplessly, her eyes shiny with tears. "Do I have any choice? It's true," she said. "Honey, you've got to come out of your shell."

"Shells are good. They protect you. Ask snails," I said. "Either way, you get stepped on."

My mother began to cry. She sat down on Helen's bed.

I went to her and put my arm around her shoulder. "I'm sorry, Momma. Please don't cry."

"Oh, Jessie," she sighed. "I'm no good anymore. I used to think I was a pretty great mom. Now I can't help you or Lucas—"

"That's not true! You're a wonderful mother! You help us all the time."

My mother shook her head. "All I do is cry. But, honey—I feel like you're slipping away. I feel like I'm losing you. I'm sorry. Look at me. I'm such an inspiration." She smoothed her hair and dried her eyes. "Now, please don't leave your friend standing at the door."

"He's not my friend."

"He was a friend of Helen's."

I could've told her the truth but she didn't need the pain. Helen had protected my parents. They never knew why Bloomfield had faded away. "No big deal," Helen said, and they'd wanted to believe her. I was the one who heard her crying in the night.

I pretended to be sleeping. I didn't know what to say. "Okay," I said. "I'll talk to Bloomfield."

"Good," Mom said. "Then I'll stop crying."

When I opened the front door, Bloomfield looked startled, stepping back as if he thought I might attack him. I leaned against the doorjamb, my arms across my chest.

"My mother said you wanted to see me."

"Yeah, I miss your friendly smile," he said.

"I wouldn't talk if I were you."

"What's that supposed to mean?"

"As usual, your mouth is on upside down."

"Well, you're not exactly the Welcome Wagon Lady."

"You're not exactly welcome," I replied.

"I didn't come over here to be insulted." Bloomfield's scowl spread to his eyes.

"Why did you come over here?"

"I wanted to talk to you."

"I have nothing to say to you, Bloomfield." A lie. I

could've screamed at him for hours, for days. I would've said, *"You bastard. Helen loved you best."*

What was the point? Helen was dead. Life goes on. But not for everyone.

Bloomfield stuffed his hands into his pockets. "Look, I want to apologize," he said.

"For what? You didn't do anything wrong. Remember?"

"I'm trying to talk but you won't listen—"

"There's nothing to talk about, so just—"

A shove cut me off in midsentence. My mother had pushed me outside and locked the door. "Why don't you two take a walk?" she called sweetly.

I couldn't believe what she'd done. "Let me in, Mom."

"I can't; I'm waxing the floors."

"I'll break a window."

"Take a hike!" she roared.

Bloomfield tucked a snicker inside a cough.

"Sure," I said. "Let's take a walk. Why not?" I would let Bloomfield make his speech of repentance and then he would leave me alone. That's what I wanted.

The sun was a topaz in the bright blue sky. Kids flew by on their bikes on the way home from school. At the corner of Harker and Winston we passed Mrs. Jensen, who was waiting for the school bus to arrive. Her little boy was run over as he got off the bus on the first day of first grade. She waits with the other mothers every afternoon, her face smooth; she never cries. If her son got off the bus today, he could be driving it. He would be twenty-five.

The breeze was brisk. Bloomfield held out his jacket. He didn't need it, he said; he had a sweater. He chucked it at me. I let it fall to the sidewalk. But after another block, I ran back and got it. The fleecy sleeves still held the warmth of his arms.

Bloomfield said, "I know what you think of me."

"If you did," I said, "you wouldn't come around."

"I was an asshole."

"On good days."

He shot me a look. "You're not supposed to agree with me."

"I can't help it; for once you're right."

He frowned. He shoved his hands in his back pockets. He looked up at the sky. "I got scared," he said finally.

"You weren't the one who was dying."

"I blew it. I was an idiot, all right? Is that what you want me to say?"

"It doesn't matter what you say now. Helen's dead."

He grabbed my arms and shouted into my face. "Did I kill her, Jess? Did I take a gun and shoot her?"

"You might as well have! She loved you!"

"Helen loved everybody!"

"Not like she loved you!"

"I didn't ask her to love me! I never told her I loved her! I liked her a lot," Bloomfield said. "I cared about Helen but—"

"—not enough to stick around!"

"Was I supposed to marry her?"

"Let go of my arms."

"Was I supposed to save her? I'm not Prince Charming! Nobody could save her, Jess!"

An army of white knights could not save Helen. They turned their backs on the field of battle and hid in the forest of her veins. No, those aren't veins; those are serpents, those are snakes, devouring strength, squeezing the life from Helen's body—

Bloomfield had to run to catch up with me, by the maze of monkey bars in the park where Helen and I had played. On the swing set children laughed and pumped their legs, climbing higher and higher into the sky.

I couldn't breathe. I had to sit down. Bloomfield collapsed on the grass beside me.

"You never mentioned you were part gazelle," he gasped. I plucked and shredded spears of grass. I had to get home. I was afraid. Of what? he would ask, if he could read my mind. I would be too ashamed to answer: *Of everything.* I'm afraid the sandbox will swallow me up. Afraid the sun will fall on me. Afraid to sleep and afraid to wake up.

There is no safe place for me.

"Jessie," Bloomfield said, "I'm sorry Helen died."

"That's nice of you."

"She was a whole lot nicer than you! Shit. I didn't mean that. I'm sorry. I'm sorry! I'm sorry about everything!" Bloomfield was crying. It sounded so painful. He fell back on the grass, clutching his chest, covering his eyes. Tears slid down his face. I stroked his hair.

Why can't bad things stop happening for one second? Just stop—so the world can be happy. Everything looks pretty, but inside it's spoiled, like that watermelon Dad got for Helen. She wasn't feeling well and he knew it would please her; Helen loved watermelon.

It was late in the season and most of the fruit stands were closed. We kept driving and driving down country roads. The longer we drove, the worse we all felt. The fun was gone; we could tell Dad was desperate, as if this mission, if successful, would cure Helen. Meanwhile, in the backseat, she's saying, "Daddy, it doesn't matter." Lucas was mad. "Dad, you're not going to find one." Mom stared out the window, silent.

My father finally found one, in a grocery store. We took it home and cut it open. It was bad. Helen insisted on eating some anyway. "This part in the middle's pretty good," she kept saying. Dad and Lucas got into an argument.

It was as if our family was captured in that rind; what had been so pink and sweet had turned bitter. The season for good times was in the past and all we could see ahead was winter.

"I'm sorry," Bloomfield said. He sat up and wiped his eyes. I never cry; my eyes are like stones. If I cried, I would die. I would drown in sorrow. Sorrow surrounds me. It fills my lungs. *Jessie's sad,* sing the songs on the radio.

Across the park, church bells began to ring. When we were children that meant it was time to go home. The kids on the swings leaped off and flew through the air, landing

in the sandbox, almost at our feet. One of them was Sara
Rose.

She walked over to me, hitching up the red tights under
her dress.

"Hi, Jessie," she said. "Where's Helen?"

She always asks me that, as if I'll finally come up with
an explanation she likes better.

"You know where she is," I said.

Sara Rose peered at me. "Is she still dead?"

I thought, I wish Helen could hear that. She'd laugh.

"Yes," I said.

"I wish she wasn't."

"Me, too."

"Come on, Sara!" her brother called. "We have to go
home!"

Sara Rose studied Bloomfield, then looked back at me.
She said, "Did Helen have a heartichoke?"

"You mean a heart attack?"

Sara Rose nodded.

"No, she had cancer."

"What's that?"

"It means she was real sick," I said.

"I know," Sara Rose said. "I miss her."

"Sara, come on! I'm leaving!" screamed her brother.

The wind whipped the curls around Sara Rose's face.
"Can you come over to my house and play?" she asked.

"Not today," I said. "Maybe soon."

"Okay!" She ran away across the grass.

Bloomfield said, "Was that a munchkin?"

"Helen used to sit for her. I sit for them sometimes, but the kids don't like me as much. Who does?"

"I'm sorry I said that."

"Everybody's sorry. What difference does it make?" I said.

The streets were full of rush-hour traffic. The cars made me nervous. They were going too fast. I kept my eyes on the sidewalk on the way home. When we got to the house I handed Bloomfield his jacket.

"Thanks for the great time. We'll have to do it again," I said.

"Is it okay if I call you?"

"Call me what?"

"Maybe we could see a movie."

"Maybe," I said. His tears had washed away my hate, but I was empty.

I knocked and my brother opened the door. "It's unlocked," he said, glaring at Bloomfield. As soon as I got inside, he said, "What's that jerk want?"

"Your autograph," I said. "He's just using me."

Later, he and Dad got into it bad. Dad started it. He got all worked up about the way Lucas was playing Helen's favorite Christmas carol, "Joy to the World."

He pounded on Lucas's bedroom door and told him to turn down the amp. Didn't Lucas have any consideration? It was a Christmas carol! Not heavy metal!

Lucas's eyes blazed. He'd play it any damn way he liked!

It was supposed to sound joyful! It was called "Joy to the World"! Joy, Dad, get it?

I hid in the living room. Mom dragged Dad downstairs. They drove off to buy a Christmas tree. I wanted to talk to my brother, but he was so angry, I was afraid.

When they left I thought he'd turn up the amp so high it would blow the house to kingdom come. But he didn't. He got out his old acoustic guitar and began to play the same carol, picking out the tune as if plucking each note from the anthem of creation; the sound the earth makes as it spins in the dark, the song of the stars in heaven.

Halfway up the stairs I sat down and listened to Lucas serenade our sister.

**II**

*My hair is falling out. My face is puffy. I am ugly. I am so ugly.*

*Bambi told Bloomfield I am wearing a wig. She told him I have cancer.*

*I am never coming out of this bedroom again. I don't even want the family to see me.*

*I have put off writing down what has happened. When I see the words on paper, I'll know they're true. I don't want to think about it. I want to pretend it never happened.*

*What's the use? Bambi told Bloomfield I have cancer. The words fell out of her big mouth. She keeps calling me up to apologize, and came over here yesterday with boohoo eyes. "I'm sorry! I'm sorry!" As if that makes any difference.*

*The carriage is a pumpkin. The bubble has shattered. The instant of enchantment is gone.*

*It's been over a week since I heard from Bloomfield. I'll probably never hear from him again.*

*Jessie wants to kill him. She wants to burn down his house. "That bastard," she says. "You're too good for him, Helen."*

*Yes, I'm such a prize, with my yellow eyes and my threadbare teddy bear hair.*

*When he called me up, I already knew what had happened, because Bambi told Jessie and Jessie told me.*

*I should've told him the truth a long time ago. So both of us are phonies. Just illusions.*

*He said, "I've been meaning to talk to you for a while, Helen, but I didn't know how to say it."*

*"Say what?" My vocal chords were stiff. The words sounded like chunks of wood.*

*"Things are getting a little too intense with you and me."*

*"Intense?" I said. "What do you mean?"*

*"Like when we went to the beach. . . . I really like you, Helen."*

*"So that's why you're calling me up to say good-bye? Because you like me so much?" I sounded mean.*

*He said, "I'm not ready to settle down with one person."*

*"No kidding." I laughed. "You think I am? I'm eighteen."*

*"That's what I mean. I'm not ready to go steady. I think it would be good if we saw some other people. For a while."*

*"Do you have anybody in mind?" Everybody knows Cheryl Prentiss still wants him. She's made that very clear to me.*

*He sighed. "I didn't call you up to argue, Helen."*

"No, you called me up to say so long. This has nothing to do with my cancer, right?"

Dead silence.

"Bambi told me she told you," I said. "What's the matter; don't you like bald women?"

"Helen—"

"Forget it. Just forget it."

"I'm sorry."

"I don't want you to be sorry! I don't need your pity!"

"This has nothing to do with your illness," Bloomfield said.

"Oh bullshit," I said. "That's a lie."

"Talk about liars! You never told me the truth!"

"Because I knew you'd do what you're doing right now! I knew you'd bail out!"

"I'm not bailing out! I just need a little space!"

"You can take all the space you want, Bloomfield! You can take all the space in the universe! I don't want you coming over here, or writing me, or calling. I just want you to leave me alone! Is that clear?"

I slammed down the phone, cutting off his voice. I'll never know what he was going to say. I'll never know if he got scared because we were getting "too intense" or because he found out that I'm dying.

I am dying. There is no escape.

Here comes my visual therapist, galloping up on her spangled stallion. She says, "Dying only takes a hot second, Helen. We're living till the last breath."

That's easy for her to say; her bones don't ache. She has all

her strength and her hair. She has the future to open like a
birthday present. She isn't trapped in a body that's betraying her.

No matter what she says, she can't save me.

I wish I could talk to Jess, but she gets scared when I'm
depressed. And the folks keep up this big cheerful front; like, if
they run fast enough, the truth won't catch up. So I feel like a
cloud at their garden party.

I know how hard this must be for them. Their baby is sick
and all they can do is stand by helplessly. Whereas I'm on the
inside, looking out, and I know how I feel, and how much I can
stand, and frankly, my dear, I can't stand it.

Sara Rose just came over. She wanted me to come out and
play, but I asked Mom to send her away. I told Mom I was
nauseated (true) and hid my eyes, so she wouldn't see Bloomfield
inside them.

I am so sick of being tired. I am so tired of being sick. I'm
dying from the feet up. My toes are always frozen. I'm sick of
being examined and stabbed and jabbed. They expect me to be
such a "good sport," as if I'd been born to be a pincushion, as
if my mission in life was dying.

My therapist charges by, hollering, "Rise above the pain!" I'm
trying but it drags me down, grabbing my ankles, grounding me.
"You're a bird, Helen! Fly!" And I rise off the pain plain, like
a plane lifting up off a flaming runway, into a blazing blue sky.

O lift me up! My God, please take me. My heart is breaking.
I want to die. I am so cold and no one will hold me. O
Bloomfield, why won't you love me?

Please love me please love me please love me.

*I am too much trouble. Revolting. Repulsive. A piece of diseased meat. I could smash my bedroom mirror and use the glass to slash my wrists, but Mom would just have to clean up the mess, which wouldn't be red, it would be green as money and stink like chemotherapy. Hold your nose and drink the poison, Helen; it might kill the cancer or it might kill you. Look on the bright side—what have you got to lose?*

*I feel so sorry for myself. This is a true extravaganza. I am wallowing in a tub of warm self-pity.*

*Damn it to hell, I have a right to be angry! Damn it to hell, I'm going to die! And I'll still be a virgin! And I won't ever have a baby! And nobody's ever going to love me most of all!*

*My God, my God, why hast thou forsaken me? I believe in you and you don't believe in me! I'm the only person in this family who isn't an atheist or a Unitarian—and you're going to kill me!*

*Why is this happening? If there's some reason or plan, could You give me a hint? It would mean a lot!*

*I want to die for something, like rescuing people, or fighting for freedom. I want there to be a reason for my life, and my death. Is that so much to ask?*

*Nobody's answering.*

*The only person I can really talk to is Ms. Tormey. She's known about the cancer for months. (Now everybody at school knows. Secrets leak out of Bambi. It's amazing she kept her mouth shut so long.)*

*Ms. Tormey listens; she doesn't flinch or change the subject. She tells me to write down my feelings on paper. She says, "Use it, Helen! Use the fear and the rage!"* Writers can't change the world, she says, but they can make poetry and laughter from pain. She is urging me to work on my book. (How to Survive Your Life *Tip #1: Don't get cancer.*). We're currently studying mythology. Next month she plans to have us become (on paper) our favorite mythological creature. Will I be a dragon? A griffin? A mermaid? I used to love unicorns until they became so cliché; there were unicorn earrings, lunch boxes, stationery; unicorns everywhere you looked. Which is funny, because the breed is so rare, you can't hunt one; it must come to you.

So I'm trying to decide which creature to be. But it's hard to care when I feel so crummy, and in the back of my mind I can't help wondering what difference it all makes.

Ms. Tormey says, *Helen, we're all going to die.*

True, but for most people, that time is way off in the future. I don't have a future. I don't even have today because Bambi Bigmouth took it all away. I don't ever want to go back to school.

O Bloomfield, why can't this all be a mistake? Why can't we start from the beginning? I would be reborn, new and healthy and strong—and still so in love with you.

News travels fast. The kids at school treat me differently. They're too nice, even the ones who never liked me. At the same time, they've all taken a step back, keeping their distance, as if death might be contagious. And I see them staring at my hair (or where my real hair used to be) and at my skinny thighs and chicken-bone wrists. You could snap me down the middle and make a wish. I am swimming in my clothes. Mom tries to get me to eat eat eat, but even the smell of food makes me sick.

*They're upset because I wouldn't go downstairs for dinner to-night.*

*I didn't have the strength for it.*

*My family needs a table-side referee, officiating, blowing his whistle. Foul! Out of bounds! Low blow! Cheap shot! Their voices carry up the stairs to my room; Lucas and Dad tearing each other into bite-sized pieces.*

*I tried to talk to Lucas about Dad the other night. He got so mad. He said, "Why do you always take his side?"*

*"I don't take anybody's side," I said. "We're supposed to be a family."*

*"That doesn't mean we are." He stomped out. In a while he came back and played some of my favorite songs on his guitar. Lucas never apologizes. Instead, he sends musical flowers.*

*He's being especially sweet to me lately. Quick: Be nice to your sister; she's dying. He doesn't need to worry; I know he loves me. He can't help it if he's such a grouch.*

*Living with Lucas is like living with a boarder; we know little about him except what he eats. Mom says he'll be married with three kids in college before she even finds out he's engaged.*

*It's hard to picture Lucas married. He hates his aloneness but he's proud of it, too. Who could pierce his fierceness? Who would dare to walk through the hurricane to its watchful eye?*

*I hope I live to meet that woman. I hope I live long enough to do something useful, to write a poem or a story that's so true it will still be alive when I'm gone.*

*O Bloomfield, I wanted to find the words that would unlock the love inside of you.*

*All I do is talk to myself on paper. I wonder if all writers are crazy. I am not a real writer. I am just a person. There's a stranger in the mirror with fat cheeks and no hair. Ugly ugly ugly, with a pooched out belly because my damn kidneys are screwing up.*

*I hear the front door slam. It sounds like Lucas's Impala is tearing up the front lawn. My father stops shouting. The TV goes on; one of those loud, unfunny comedies.*

*Jessie just came to the bedroom door and shook the handle. (It's locked.) I told her I was finishing some writing. My eyes are puffy. I cannot stop crying. When I think of Bloomfield, my heart twists inside me, like an injured animal lying on the road. Finish it off. Don't let it suffer. Pain is not the same thing as love.*

*O Bloomfield! I love you! I'm sorry I'm so ugly! Kiss me again! Breathe your life into my body! Heal me with your love!*

*I'm such a joke.*

*Look at me. God. Why can't I turn back the clock? Let me try, in my mind, going back to the time when we walked on the beach and he held me in his arms and he told me: Helen, you're so special.*

*Turn down the light so it glows, not glares. The curtains are drawn; no one is staring. If I stand just so in front of the mirror, my face is hidden. I see only my body, my hideous body, my faithless flesh, my naked belly that blossoms like an egg. I pretend I am pregnant. There is a baby inside me. O Lord, for one second give me peace, give me hope. Let me dream that I am full of life.*

## 12

TODAY WAS HELEN'S BIRTHDAY. DECEMBER TENTH. SHE would've been nineteen.

We went out to dinner. We're so conspicuous; Lucas and Dad arguing about everything and nothing, constantly.

The first thing they argued about was where to eat. Lucas wanted Mexican food, Dad wanted Italian. Mom suggested the International Kitchen.

We went to Ming's. Chinese food was Helen's favorite. Dad ordered a Shirley Temple for me and asked Lucas if he wanted one too.

"I'm twenty, Dad, not ten!" Lucas ordered coffee.

"Isn't this nice?" Mom said, trying to make it that way. "The first time we brought you children here—" She launched into a beloved family fable. When the waiter filled twelve-year-old Helen's water glass, she drank it all down, so he refilled it. So she drank that glass, and the next one, and the next one, until my parents intervened. She didn't want to hurt the waiter's feelings, she'd explained.

My mother's eyes danced as she told that story, but Dad's face had gotten sad. He interrupted Mom when she started to talk about how cute Helen was as a baby.

"How's school, Jess?"

"Fine." He doesn't need to know I'm flunking math.

"That's good. School's so important, honey. I know you don't realize that now, but someday when you're all grown up—"

He thinks I'm a baby. He did the same thing with Helen. It drove her crazy. He didn't want her to date. He didn't want her to drive. On the rare occasions when she had a guy over, Dad managed to be lurking in the background, reading the newspaper, tinkering with the car.

He got worse as Helen did. So did the arguments with Lucas. They fought about the chemotherapy. Dad thought it was Helen's only hope; Lucas thought it was just another way to die.

One night while Helen was in the hospital, Dad and Lucas started fighting at dinner.

"If she's got to have the chemotherapy, she could at least smoke grass," Lucas said.

"It's illegal," my father said flatly.

"For God's sake, Dad! It's medically proven! She wouldn't feel like shit all the time. It relieves the side effects."

"It's out of the question! I won't have Helen becoming addicted to drugs!"

"She doesn't have time to become addicted!" Lucas shouted.

My father reached across the table and slapped him hard. My mother cried out and put her hands to her face. Lucas sat there, stunned, his eyes filling with tears. Then he ran out of the house.

"Lucas, wait!" Dad ran after him but it was too late. Lucas didn't come home for several days.

The waiter brought our Chinese food; steaming platters heaped on a tray. But as soon as I smelled it, I was full. My father kept talking, talking, talking, filling Helen's empty chair with words.

"How's the band coming, Luke?"

"What band?"

"I thought you were getting a band together."

"I thought so, too. It fell through."

People come by our house with drums and guitars and take over the living room. But it never works out; they're into drugs or drinking but not rehearsing. Lucas is too good for his own good.

"Most of them are into club music," Lucas said.

"Club music," Dad said. "What's that mean?"

"The kind of music you play in dinner clubs. To make money."

"There's nothing wrong with making money," Dad said.

"Depends how you make it."

"What's that supposed to mean?"

"Mmmm, isn't the lemon chicken good!" my mother said.

"It means I'm not into playing Top Forty so a bunch of polyester heads can freak out on Friday night."

Dad said, "Sometimes you have to give a little. The name of the game is compromise."

"I don't play games. Or clubs," Lucas said.

I pushed the food around on my plate.

Home again, Mom brought out a cake she'd made. No candles. We sat around and ate it and talked about everything except what we were thinking. Then Mom got out the home movies: Helen and me on the swings, Helen and me in the May Day parade. Lucas suddenly had to go someplace, and Dad went to bed; he felt real tired.

I sat in the dark with Mom and watched Helen dance and laugh and wave. My mother drank a lot of wine.

Bambi came by and we went up to my room and she showed me her new red and blue tattoo; her boyfriend's initials just above her left breast.

"Promise you won't tell!" she said, as if anybody was interested. Sorry, but I'm going to have to go to the *Enquirer*. This is news. This is big, Bambi, big.

She said, "My boyfriend's asked me to marry him."

"You're kidding."

That hurt her feelings. Bambi's built like a tank but she breaks like china.

"I mean," I said, "you're not pregnant, are you?"

"Of course not. But he loves me a lot, I think."

"Do you love him?"

She twirled a strand of her limp black hair. She said, "He's nice to me." She got out a Band-Aid box full of marijuana.

"You can't smoke that here," I said. "My mother would smell it." She was downstairs watching all the movies again.

"You could tell her it was incense."

"I don't want to get stoned." Dope makes Bambi feel sleepy and happy, but it fine-tunes my pain. I see things too clearly. I remember things I want to forget.

"What's this?" Bambi had picked up Helen's journal. Seeing her touch it upset me. I held out my hand until she gave it to me.

"Helen's journal. I've been reading it," I said.

"Is there good stuff in it?"

"Like what? Like sex?"

"Yeah, did she and Bloomfield ever do it?"

I'd be damned if I'd let Bambi into Helen's mind.

"If she did, do you think I'd tell you?"

"Why not? I was her friend."

"Then you know," I said.

"Come on," Bambi pouted. "You're holding."

"It's mostly about her writing. There's some poems and stuff."

"Maybe you could publish it post . . . post . . ." Bambi wracked her brain for the right word. "Maybe you could publish it posthumorously."

"What?"

"You know; after her death."

That cracked me up. Helen would've laughed, too.

"You mean posthumously."

"So? I was close." Bambi's face was red. "Why do you always make fun of me, Jess?"

"I don't."

"You do. You're always laughing at me."

"I can't help it when you say something stupid."

"How am I supposed to know how to pronounce it? I'm not a big brain like you! Helen was smart too, but she was real nice!" Bambi made a tearful exit.

"Helen was a saint!" I roared down the stairs. "What a shame I didn't die instead of her! Helen was everybody's favorite favorite!"

She was my favorite favorite too.

I look for her everywhere; in strangers' faces, seeking that warm, shy smile. I go to Foothill Park and climb our hill to the top. To the south, north, and east, miles of civilization; to the west, mountains rolling to the silver ocean. The wind makes my eyes tear and I think of Helen, her brown hair kiting in the breeze. "Jess," she would say with a happy sigh. "It's so beautiful here. Let's never come down."

I haven't been there lately. Riding in the car scares me. I almost caused an accident the other day. Thinking a bus was going to hit us, I grabbed Mom's arm. My legs shake badly and my foot keeps pumping an imaginary brake.

Life is full of risks, Jessie, Dr. Shubert says. You mustn't let fear overtake you.

Week after week I visit her office. We are making a study

of each other. Her stylish clothes and manicured nails reflect a polished professional. She means well, but we're not making progress. Instead of becoming closer, I am moving away. She is running along shouting beside my window while the train is leaving the station.

Dr. Shubert says I'm trying to punish myself because I'm still alive and Helen isn't.

She says that I am idealizing Helen, as often happens when a loved one dies. Remembering the good times and burying the bad.

No, I remember. Especially the mood swings. That happened right around the end. I'd walk into the room and Helen would land on me, raving about something I'd done.

"Well, why don't you have a fit about it, Helen? I'm sorry I wore your stupid blouse!"

"My stupid blouse!" She grabbed it from me and tore it apart. "My stupid blouse doesn't fit anymore because my stupid stomach sticks out! Stupid, stupid—" She ripped her clothes out of the closet. She tipped over the bookcase. I begged her to stop. I'm so sick of myself! I'm sorry!" she cried, collapsing, exhausted. "I'm sorry, Jessie! I'm sorry!"

Listen to me, Jessie, Dr. Shubert says, surviving Helen's death doesn't mean you're abandoning her. She wouldn't want you to be sad; she would want you to be happy. Life goes on and so must you.

I have hidden the extent of my guilt from Dr. Shubert. Saying the words aloud would kill me.

I would not let Helen talk to me. When she needed me,

I turned away. I didn't want to hear about her pain and her fear. I didn't want to see her changing.

I was too scared and selfish to reach out to my sister.

It is not only Bloomfield who betrayed her.

## 13

MAY 7

*I'm in the hospital at the moment, awaiting a transfusion. Boy, am I sick of this place. But a batch of new blood should make me feel a lot better. As soon as I'm done, I can go home. Hurray!*

*From my window I can see the bright blue sky, with clouds like a herd of white buffaloes. It's one of those blustery spring days when the sun keeps flirting and hiding its face, then popping out, promising summer.*

*The little girl in the next bed reminds me of Sara Rose, with the same bright eyes and puckered up mouth, as if she's about to tell a joke. Her name is Darcy. We played a game of Sorry awhile ago (she flattened me) and whenever she'd bump me off the board, she'd shriek, "Sorry, old chum!" giggling like a chimpanzee.*

*Her parents visited this morning, trying not to act scared, but you could see the fear in their eyes. After they left, Darcy said, "Some people just can't take it, Helen," as if she were ninety instead of nine. Her folks wouldn't worry so much if they'd seen her eat lunch, all of hers, then most of mine.*

*I am trying to catch up on my schoolwork and journal. I took a nosedive after Bloomfield's departure. Now it seems silly that I got so upset, but breaking up was awful. He'd see me in the halls and nod his head . . . as if we'd met, once upon a time, and he remembered my face but not my name.*

*He's the most frightened person I've ever met, afraid that if he cares about something, he might get hurt. That's why he acts so blasé, so cool.*

*I feel sorry for him. (I am such a fool.) He reminds me of Lucas. They both go around in a self-imposed fury, faces frozen in a scowl as if telling the world: I don't care if you love me! I don't love you first!*

*Good luck, Bloomfield, little rabbit, little darling. And good luck to Cheryl Prentiss and all the others (like me), who will think they can unlock his heart when Bloomfield holds the key.*

*Don't look back. Sadness makes you weak. I must move ahead. I must be strong.*

*I got a wonderful letter from Ms. Tormey and the class, and lots of get-well cards from kids at school. It surprises me; I've always been so shy. I didn't think anybody noticed me. The cards make it sound like I'm rebounding from the flu: "Hurry up and get well soon!" That sort of thing. People don't know what to say about cancer. It ain't considered polite to write: "I hope you don't die."*

*Anyway, I've decided I'm going to live—long enough to be a FABULOUS success and grind my enemies to dust beneath my feet. Long enough to own a dog and name him Bloomfield. . . .*

*Now, Helen June: It's not nice to be mean.*

*True, but meanness gives you spunk and juice and tastes so much sweeter than sorrow!*

*The nurse just took another blood sample. What in blazes do they do with the stuff? Is this place called Transylvania General? Maybe Dracula wasn't a vampire, just a misguided lab technician.*

*I'm feeling tired today, but happy.*

*For one thing, I'll be home soon. It's springtime and millions of flowers are blooming and I want to plant a vegetable garden.*

*For another thing, I'll graduate from high school next month. THEN what? I wish I knew. I guess in the fall I'll go to the J. C., and then eventually I'll major in English. Get a teaching certificate so I'll have a way to eat while I'm waiting to hit the Big Time.*

*I don't expect I'll ever be a Famous Writer but I'm sure going to try to be good. Not that I have a choice; I HAVE to do it; like birds gotta fly and Lucas gotta argue. It's destiny. It's in the blood.*

*No matter WHOSE blood I have. I have to write.*

*Here's a poem for the culture section of* How to Survive Your Life:

## *Hope*

When you love someone
you give him the key
to your heart.
You hope
that he won't come in and
wreck the place.

You hope
that he will
feel what you feel;
see what you see.
It's like trying to meet for lunch
in a dream.

It is so unlikely
that you will
feed each other's needs;
follow each other's leads;
that you hope that,
if you can't come out of this
together,
you'll come out of this
alive.

*So relax, Bloomfield. I survived you—although it was nip and tuck for awhile. I put on this happy face (see illustration:* ☺ *)*

*for Ma and Pa, meanwhile threatening to slash my wrists in the privacy of my/our bedroom every night. Jessie puts up with a lot. My moods go up and down. It's partly the cancer and partly the chemo, and partly my giant crush on Bloomfield, which turned around and crushed me flat.*

*Sometimes I don't get the meaning of life. It's like trying to put together a giant puzzle with half the pieces lost under the couch.*

*Then I'll experience a flash of understanding; realization breaks through my brain, like the time when I was little and I noticed that I had to keep swallowing spit all the time.*

*Monumental breakthroughs like that.*

*Once in a while I'll wake up and think: Wow, I'm alive right now! The hugeness of the universe sweeps me to the stars. Billions of stars! Millions of people! Trucks down the freeway and blood through my veins! Dinosaurs! Astronauts! Languages! Money! Money's so weird; it's just paper symbols, like hearts on Valentine's Day. Or the musical symbols that encode symphonies. Or the words that build worlds on pages.*

*For that second I'll feel as if I'm part of everything, and that everything that exists is part of me. All the lost puzzle pieces fall into place, and life makes sense, and God is love and peace.*

*Lucas goes CRAZY when I say stuff like that! Sometimes when the phone rings, he gets it and says, "Helen, it's for you. It's God. Hold on, please. She's been expecting your call."*

*Lucas claims that he doesn't believe in anything. But I think he sees God as some heavenly hit man; a celestial sniper firing at the frightened mob below.*

*That's not what I believe but I have no answers for Lucas. Most of the time I'm lost in the fog, feeling my way home.*

*I just got a phone call (from Jessie, not God). She really cracked me up. She said Lucas and Dad are playing golf together. Do you think it's safe to let them use clubs? she asked. Will Dad come home and say Lucas drowned in a sand trap?*

*I wish she would let people outside the family know her. She denies that she's shy and says people are jerks. She's beautiful and funny and she thinks she's ugly. Why can't she see herself clearly?*

*We talked about the time when Lucas was little and he screamed in Dad's ear to wake him up. It was funny when kids did it on TV. Dad almost had a stroke. He shot out of bed and chased Lucas down the street— Now it's a family joke. I can still see Lucas hauling down the block, barefoot, in his pajamas. . . .*

*Nurse Vampira is back with my transfusion.*

*I say, "Fill 'er up with unleaded, please."*

## 14

WE MADE IT THROUGH CHRISTMAS. IT WAS WORSE THAN
Thanksgiving. Christmas is such a production. And you
know you're supposed to be feeling happy . . . and when
you don't, you feel so wrong.

Lucas didn't even stick around on Christmas Eve. He
took off to visit friends. He slept in late the next morning
until I finally had to wake him up.

"Oh God," he groaned.

"Merry Christmas," I said.

"Yeah, fabulous." He looked hungover.

We sat around the tree and opened our presents, then ate
the special breakfast that Mom makes every Christmas.

No one could think of a thing to say.

The day dragged on for years.

Dr. Shubert says that, when someone dies, it's hard to

survive the "firsts": the first Thanksgiving and Christmas without them, their birthday, and the anniversary of their death.

She's right, of course, but being right doesn't help. Dr. Shubert calls me her client, not her patient. She tries to relate but she dated Freud. Half the time she doesn't understand what I am saying.

Me: . . . so then Lucas split.

Dr. S: You mean your brother left the house?

No, he split down the middle like a threadbare schizo; tore in half like a fraying manic. He and Dad said killing things. My brother shouted, "You always make me feel like a jerk!" Then Dad said, "That's not true! I love you!" The words hung in the air while we stared at them. "I know," Lucas said. He looked embarrassed and confused. Then he split.

I've been staying up too late. I've got bags under my eyes. Overnight bags. Get it?

Hey, dja hear about the woman who had six months to live? She freaks out; she says: "Doc, what can I do?" He tells her to marry a big fat guy and move into a trailer park. "Will that lengthen my life?" the woman asks. "No," the doctor says, "but it'll seem longer."

When you watch TV at one A.M., your mind fills up with video confetti.

I am enjoying Christmas vacation. I am glad to be out of school. There's a history report I'm supposed to be working on. . . . It's around the house someplace.

The Big Bambino called awhile ago, raving about her boyfriend the meathead. He did this hilarious thing on New Year's Eve; put balloons under his sweater and pretended to be a girl. The man is a comic genius.

Bloomfield invited me to a New Year's Eve party but I didn't want to see him.

Bloomfield is a mirror reflecting the conspirator in a crime of silence against Helen.

So I baby-sat for Sara Rose and her brothers. They wanted to stay up and welcome in the new year, but midnight was way too late. So we pretended we were in New York City and pushed ahead the time by three hours. Instant celebration! The kids threw cornflakes into the air and banged pots and pans together.

Helen sat for them last New Year's Eve. She was winding down her baby-sitting. She didn't have time; she was interested in guys. Helen sure was changing. Sometimes I resented her. Especially when she tried to leave me behind. How can the left foot walk without the right? Who has been left behind and who has moved ahead? Does heaven exist? Can you see me, Helen?

O Helen, why can't I see you?

I don't think I'm going to baby-sit for a while. I really don't need the money. And lately, when I talk to people, sometimes I feel funny. I can't look in their eyes and my face gets stiff and hot, and my words tumble out in hopeless clots. Especially with grown-ups but even with kids, who nail you with their lie-detector eyes. That's why Bambi doesn't like them. She says they're pains. When she was little her mom would dump her at the library, then go shopping in San Francisco. Bambi would be there all day. Unfortunately, instead of absorbing literature, she'd do stuff like photocopying her face.

I want to leave this house. I want to go away. I want to become someone else.

Does reading Helen's journal help me or make me feel worse? Sometimes it's too close to call. It's as if Helen were talking to me! She sounds so near! If only she could hear me, too. There's so much I would say. Like: We meant to go to Disneyland again. We didn't think you'd die so soon. One minute you're alive and the next, you're memory. Life is so fragile it scares me, Helen. My heart is so full it might burst. Full of love and fear. Children die every second. Burned or drowned or starved or neglected; stolen and strangled and worse.

In the country of lost children, are you queen, Helen?

I want to kill myself so I'll stop thinking, but I'm too afraid that dying would hurt.

I have got to get myself together. I think Mom knows I've been cutting school. Some mornings she just lets me sleep. Most nights I wrestle dreams and lose.

Last night Helen and I were at Frontier Village. It looked exactly like it did before it got torn down for a subdivision; with the phony jail and saloon, and the merry-go-round, and the make-believe gunfights at noon.

The day was sunny and the booths and rides were

mobbed by happy children and their parents. Helen and I were having fun. We were playing tag. Then I was it and Helen hid.

At first it was funny. "Helen? Where are you?" Then I was running through the crowd. People's faces had changed; their smiles were wreaths of teeth wrapped around their heads.

I looked everywhere. I couldn't find Helen.

The day leaked away. All the people went home. I was alone. Trash was blowing in the wind, down streets that would soon be covered with tract homes as fake as Frontier Village.

Tonight I tried to tell Lucas about the dream, and he said, "Let's go hear some music."

"Where?"

"San Carlos."

"I can't."

"Why not?" Lucas looked exasperated. "These guys are really good."

"I'm sure they are. I just don't feel like going."

Lucas shook his head and left my room. Then he came back in and shut the door.

He said, "You know what's happening, don't you, Jess. You're not so dumb that you don't."

"What're you talking about?"

"Helen's dead! Nothing can change that! You're letting this whole thing swallow you up!"

I almost started to cry. "Don't you think I know that?"

"What're you going to do, hole up in here forever? Take correspondence courses for life? You're afraid to go out of this goddamn house! You hardly even leave this room! When was the last time you went outside?"

"I don't have to answer you!"

He stepped into the hallway, then looked back at me. "Listen to me, Jessie, you can't outrun it. You have to face what's chasing you."

"If you're so smart, how come you're so screwed up?" I slammed the door on my brother.

Lucas thundered down the stairs. Moments later, he roared off in his Impala. In the silence that followed I heard my father say to my mother, "What now?"

I ask myself this question.

## 15

MAY 15

*I AM SO GLAD TO BE HOME!*

*I could do cartwheels down the street!*

*The whole damn world looks good enough to eat!*

*It is one of those STUPENDJUS spring days, faultless as a child, one of whom happens to be standing beside me. Let's see what Sara Rose would like to record for posterity.*

*S.R.: "What for?"*

*Me: "This is my journal. I'm writing down all the things I'm thinking."*

*S.R.: "Why don't you just tell them to me?"*

*Good point. So I tell her that I've never been more content than I am at this moment, on this warm May morning. Sara Rose says: "GOOD!" and barks like a dog, then goes back to stirring the applesauce we're cooking on her Heather Homemaker Elec-*

*tric Toy Stove, beneath the blooming snowball tree.*

*I have been home for about a week now and have never felt better in my life. It's funny how quickly things can change; one second I'm jumping out the window, the next, I'm admiring the view. I should do what Dad says and stay in the present. I sap (sap's the word) my strength with worry about what might happen in the future.*

*I can only live one day at a time. And this day is as bright as something Sara Rose would color with the crayons she hasn't eaten.*

*Also, I'm feeling very creative, which always does me good. One of my poems ("Leaving Home") will appear in the yearbook. Ms. Tormey surprised me with that news yesterday. She thinks I did an excellent job on the mythological creatures paper. I chose the phoenix. The bird consumes itself in fire, then rises anew from its ashes. The piece was written from the phoenix's perspective, just prior to its death/rebirth. Ms. Tormey says my ability to empathize is what makes me such a good writer.*

*I'd better get a grip on this brag festival.*

*Anyway, I'm really pleased.*

*Mom looks a lot better than she did a while back. When I'm sick, she looks how I feel. Sometimes I worry about what will happen to her if anything happens to me. She'll still have Jessie—but who will Jessie have?*

*Nope. I'm not going to think like that. Onward and upward!*

*Oh, can you smell that applesauce bubbling? My tastebuds are blooming with longing.*

*Or, to be more specific and less poetic: I'm practically drooling.*

*Speaking of eating: Bambi & I went out to lunch this week. Talk about a treat! She doesn't stop talking while she's chewing (or doing anything else, for that matter), so you get these great Technicolor close-ups of her burger being pummeled to a pulp. . . . She'd just bought a vat of some industrial-strength complexion cleanser that she claimed would give her a brand new face. Her mom calls any kind of skin cream "beauty goo." We went over there one time and she was rubbing yogurt into her face; not plain white yogurt, the kind with fruit. Another time— I'll never forget this—I walked into the bathroom and Mrs. Bordtz was sitting in the empty tub, naked, eating a pomegranate. Bright red juice was all over the place. It looked like the scene of a chainsaw massacre.*

*She said, "This way I don't get the juice on my clothes."*

*God bless the Bordtzes! They make my family look normal by comparison.*

*I wrote a song for Lucas. He actually likes it! It actually made him laugh!*

*We've been getting along so well lately. He's really been nice, asking how I'm doing and making me tea, etc. We went out and heard some music last night (Jessie sulked 'cause she wasn't invited. Why can't he and I do stuff together, just like Jessie and I do?)*

*This really neat thing happened at the club. The band asked Lucas to sit in. So he got up and played a couple of songs; rhythm and blues, I guess you'd call it, and everybody clapped like mad. I was so proud! I felt like shouting, "That's my brother!"*

*On the way home we stopped for coffee and I don't know what came over me; all of a sudden in the middle of nothing, I blurted, "I love you, Lucas. I just want you to know."*

*He almost dropped his coffee mug. He didn't know where to look. He nodded his head and said, "Thanks. I'm glad."*

*He wanted to say he loves me, too, but he couldn't. That's all right.*

*Here's the number one song I wrote for Lucas. (Jessie rates it a distinct number two.)*

## She Took Me to the Cleaners of Love

She was young, just seventeen,
But she looked like a million in her jeans.
From that very first night
It was love at first sight
When she took me to the cleaners of love.

Chorus:
She stole my heart, my tape deck, and my color TV.
There's a pain where my wallet used to be.
Love didn't come for free, oh no.
When she took me to the cleaners of love.

I loved her style and she loved to steal.
I knew from the start our love was real.
Everything was all right
When she turned out the lights
And took me to the cleaners of love.

Chorus: She stole my heart, etc.

O Wanda, Wanda, you took me for a ride,
And you took my Buick and my credit cards, besides.
It was love at first sight
From that very first night
When you took me to the cleaners of love.

*Lucas has worked up a tune that's JUST RIGHT and sings it like his tie was caught in an elevator door.*

*Sara Rose is handing me a steaming bowl. "Try it, Helen! It's good!"*

*It is better than good. It is sensational. This is how apples should taste on the tree: warm and tart with a cinnamon kiss, a kiss as tender as somebody's lips— Remember, Helen: Hold onto the present. The present is all there will ever be. The past is a shadow. You cannot catch it.*

*And really, who could ask for more than this perfect day, this balloon of a tree rising into the cloudless sky, this darling child beside me, saying, "Do you like it, Helen? Is it good, Helen?" as if my word were the stamp of God's approval.*

*I say, "This applesauce is the best stuff I've ever eaten."*

*"In your whole life?"*

*"In my whole life."*

*"I know." Sara Rose beams. "Me, too."*

## 16

I HAVE ASCENDED TO THE TOWER. THE TRANSITION IS COM-
plete. From my bedroom window I study the world.

I have not left this house for two weeks.

Every hour or two (or so it seems), my mother drops by
my room to weep, Pop pops by to plead, and Lucas sits on
my bed, shaking his head, kind of smiling.

"What're you going to do for the rest of your life, Jess?
Send out for Chinese food? You have to fight this thing!"

"I'm sick of fighting," I say calmly. "I'm even sick of
fighting with you."

"C'mon." He stands by the bedroom door, holding out
his hand. "I'll take you for a ride. Wherever you want to
go."

"I want to see Helen."

Saying stuff like that guarantees that he'll leave me alone.

He gallops downstairs and out the front door . . . now he's revving the Impala's engine.

"You're blowing it, Jess!" he yells at my window, then peels backward out of the driveway.

The afternoon sun spills into the room. The house is as still as a photograph.

It's three o'clock and school has let out. Children bounce down the sidewalk like rubber balls. Soon Sara Rose will be on the front lawn. Every afternoon she calls:

"Jess-sie-ee! Jess-sie-ee! Can you come out and play?"

She calls until I answer. "What is it, Sara?"

She squinches her eyes to see me. "Can you come out and play?"

"Sometime soon," I say.

"When? Tomorrow?"

"I don't know," I say.

"Can't you come to my house?" This is the stubbornest kid.

"I have to stay here," I tell her.

"Is your mom making you stay in your room?"

"Not exactly." It's too hard to explain. "I have to go now, Sara Rose. I'll see you later." I closed the window and stepped out of view. For a long time she kept looking up, waiting. Finally she went home.

Today's project: Eat more food. My shoulder blades are like skeleton wings. My wrist bones rattle. My face is too thin.

Food embarrasses me. What's the point of eating when

it comes back out, and what doesn't is used to build a body that began to wither at birth?

My body is erasing itself. The smaller I am, the less of me there is to hurt.

But I can't bear the horror in my mother's eyes. "Don't do this, Jessie. You're killing me," she said, when I left the dinner table last night.

It's funny how this whole thing started. I didn't get up one morning and decide that I would never again leave the house.

It sneaked up on me when I wasn't looking, like when you're sitting in your room reading a really good book, and the day slips away and you don't even notice until it's too dark to see the page. It reminds me of when I was twelve and we'd rented a cabin on Bass Lake. Every day we'd plunge into the icy water and swim out to a raft, where we'd sun ourselves until we were ready to jump in and cool off.

This one afternoon Mom stood on the shore, calling, "Come on out, Jessie. You've been in the water long enough." As usual, I ignored her. I was having too much fun to stop.

The water was so cold I never felt my muscles numb. When I dove off the raft that last time and began to swim toward Mom, I realized I had exhausted my strength. I would never make it back to shore.

Helen saw me. Helen saved me.

This house thing crept up on me like that. I'd been having

those panic attacks but not all the time; unpredictably. Suddenly, wherever I was, I'd have to leave. I couldn't breathe. Like that time at the supermarket. Talk about embarrassing. People probably thought I was on drugs.

I was still going to school. Well, usually. Sometimes Bambi and I would just cruise. Also, the dreams kept me up at night so in the morning I would sleep through the alarm. . . .

It's been gradual, more like wading into quicksand than jumping off the roof.

My parents have abandoned hope that this is a phase I am going through.

Last night my father said, "If you're not going to go to school, you'll finish your studies at home!" He was angry because he doesn't know what to do. He's frightened by the person I'm becoming.

A crazy person. A certified nut. Like those people who are afraid of fog, or the color red, or dairy products. One of the joys of having a shrink is that you learn about phobias and neuroses.

Dr. Shubert says (over the telephone; she refuses to come to the house) that I'm not crazy or neurotic or even long-term phobic. She says that grief is a chronic disease. "It never quite goes away, Jessie. You learn to live with the loss, and go on." She insists on treating me in her office, and has been holding my appointment time open, in case I decide to appear.

I'm afraid she'll be waiting for a long time. Each day that

passes is a nail in the front door. I'm safe here (except in case of flood, fire, famine, earthquake, or nuclear war). I've got a grocery bag stuffed with newspaper clippings of disasters from around the world; freak accidents of every description: tramplings, electrocutions, raining jet fuel; not to mention the intentional catastrophes: executions, bombings, poisoned candy.

I am cutting out death and containing it neatly.

What is happening to me?

My mother has spread the rumor at school that I'm down with pneumonia and will be back soon. She's brought all my books and assignments home. When I'm not busy studying, or cataloging calamity, I talk on the phone with Bambi Sue.

"Geez, Jess," she bleats for the nine hundredth time, "how can you stand to just sit in that room?"

"I find it helpful in preparing for my future career. I'm thinking of becoming a nun."

"Reeeeeally?" she squeals. "You're kidding!"

"You've heard about the nuns who pray for peace all the time? I'm joining an order that worries about the future twenty-four hours a day."

"You're kidding. Aren't you?"

"Always," I said. "My life is a complete joke."

Phone conversations get boring fast when (like me) you've got nothing new to say but (like Bambi) say it anyway. When Helen and I were little we called up boys. Anonymously, of course. We'd say stuff like, "We know somebody who likes you," that someone being Helen or I.

The boys would laugh and say, "Who is this, anyway?" until their moms took over the phone and announced, "Young ladies do not call young gentlemen."

I've got to get out of here. I want to go to Foothill Park. I want to see Helen's meadow. The rain has grown the hills so green. The flowers will soon go wild. I'd like to climb the hill and lie down in the grass and let the warm breeze bathe my face. I would close my eyes and see Helen again: laughing, healthy, happy, saying, "Jessie, it's so beautiful here! Let's never come down."

But I can't get there because I'm afraid to ride in cars, because I'm afraid I'll be killed. "Why are you afraid to die?" Lucas yells. "You're even more afraid to live!"

The dreams have changed. I hardly ever see Helen. They're mostly made up of sickening sensations; I'm spinning, falling, with nothing to grab onto. No walls. No floors. Utter darkness. Dr. Shubert tells me I must say, "This is a dream. I'm waking up now." But that usually doesn't work. The worst times are when I think I've woken up but I'm still dreaming. Last night I thought I ran into the kitchen and told Mom I'd been having a nightmare, and she said, "You give me such a pain," and walked out.

Then we were at Helen's funeral, in a purple room full of strangers. In the middle of the service I stood up and said, "This isn't right!" Everybody gaped at me with pale fish faces.

It wasn't right that Helen was dead. She was not a funeral kind of person. She'd never been to one in her life. The senior class dedicated their graduation ceremony to her. We talked about having a memorial when everybody in the family was up to it.

We haven't been up to it so far.

I think: What difference would it make? A ceremony won't change a thing and would just make everyone sad. But remembering Helen doesn't have to be sad. We can still be glad she was alive. It would please her to have her friends and family together; someplace pretty, like Foothill Park, with tasty refreshments and good music. Lucas could play his guitar.

It would be so *Helen* she would almost be there.

My mother just knocked on the door to announce that Bloomfield is downstairs and wishes to see me. Should she send him up?

"Over my dead body."

"It would do you good to see your friends." She tries to sound firm but her chin is quivering.

"Bloomfield is not my friend," I say.

"He was your sister's friend. She wouldn't like you to treat him this way."

"He dumped Helen when he found out she had cancer."

Why did I say that? I am so ashamed. The words leave wounds in my mother's eyes, but she refuses to be driven away.

"I'm sending him up."

"Go ahead," I say. "I'll take off all my clothes."

Before I finish unbuttoning my blouse, my mother has slammed out of the room. I pick up a sociology book and try not to think about Bloomfield.

"Rapunzel, Rapunzel, let down your hair, so that I may climb the golden stair! Come on, Rapunzel. We know you're in there. We've got the place surrounded."

It's Bloomfield, on the front lawn, making an ass of himself.

I ignore him. He continues to yell. I lean out the window. He's smiling.

I say, "How would you like a rapunzel in the mouth?"

"Sounds yummy."

I start to shut the window.

"Hey!" he shouts. "I've heard of playing hard to get, but this is ridiculous. What do you want me to do, scale the house?"

"Only if you'll promise to fall on your head."

"I'll do my best!" He runs into the garage and returns with a ladder, which he leans against the house. Bloomfield begins to climb toward my window.

I think: If only Helen could see this. It would make her laugh so hard.

"Look," I say, "if you don't get out of here, I'm going to call the police."

"Please, allow me. Police! Police!" Bloomfield cocks an ear. "I guess they didn't hear me."

"I don't know why you're doing this, Bloomfield."

"I missed your bubbly personality."

"Well, I didn't miss you. Did my mother put you up to this?"

He stopped climbing and smiled. "She said she'd give me ten bucks if I'd fall in love with her daughter."

"You don't love me."

"She only had five. But I like you a lot."

"Get out of here, Bloomfield."

"Aren't you going to invite me in?" Four feet below my window he looked up with a grin. His cap slipped off the back of his head. "Hey, you know what this reminds me of? Romeo and Juliet. 'Oh, Romeo, Romeo! wherefore art thou Romeo?' Go ahead, that's your line."

"Drop dead."

"No, that doesn't come till later. Don't you remember?" He sighed when I still didn't smile. "Why are you making this so hard, Jessie?"

"That's how you made it for Helen."

He hung his head, then looked up at me. "What do you want from me? Blood, Jess? I can't bring her back. I wish I could. Do you think hiding out here is going to help? You're just going down the tubes."

"That's my problem."

"It's your family's, too. Have you looked at your mother lately?"

"Thank God you're here to save the day."

Bloomfield shook his head. "You're a tough nut to crack."

The nut was cracking. Tears were gathering behind the eyes I willed dry.

"I'll see you tomorrow night," Bloomfield said. "Your mother has invited me to join you for dinner."

"I won't be coming to the table."

"We'll be eating in your room? Fabulous. That sounds so romantic!"

Bloomfield blew me a kiss and climbed down the ladder. He put it back in the garage and drove off in his car, all so swiftly that, in a matter of minutes, he began to seem like something I'd imagined.

## 17

MAY 26

*There's no telling what will come out of my mouth lately. I'm liable to say anything. Dr. Yee says the mood swings are side effects from all the medication. It makes me feel so snarly.*

*I mean, here's Jessie, drooping and moaning because she's so TIRED and she HAS A HEADACHE! Poor baby! She should see how it feels to be me for awhile. No, no, I wouldn't wish that on anyone, least of all my baby sister, whom I love more than life itself!!—and yet could sock in the mouth sometimes.*

*I am acting so crabby. I can't stand myself! I apologized to Jess for blowing up at her when she borrowed my boots without asking. Once I started screaming, I couldn't shut my mouth. Her eyes got wider and wider. . . .*

*I hate being pushed around by the chemo. I want to be in*

*control. The last time I sat for Sara Rose, my eyes filled up with tears for no reason.*

*"What's the matter, Helen?" She stared at me.*

*"Nothing," I blubbered. "I'm just feeling kind of sad."*

*"I know what you mean." Sara Rose stroked my hair. "Sometimes I feel that way, too. But in a little while, you'll be happy again."*

*It's true. But I'm tired of being a human Yo-Yo; up and down, up and down. I tell Dr. Yee, a hundred years from now chemo will sound as effective as applying leeches, or strapping a chicken on my body for the cancer to eat.*

*She agrees. In the meantime it's all we've got.*

*I feel repulsive when I whine like this but sometimes I'm— just sorry for myself. I try to confine my complaining to these pages and convince my mother that I'm swell. Because she and Daddy go crazy when I'm sick. They can't handle it.*

*The worst thing about sickness is that it makes you so selfish. It closes around you like a circle. You don't have the energy for anything outside. All you care about is how you feel.*

*I don't have time for this! I want to meet the world!*

*I wish I felt more like writing. I write best when I'm on fire, when there's something I've GOT to say. Lately all I want to say is, "Waaaa, I'm tired!" Most of my juice goes into schoolwork. I'm determined to get good grades. After the J.C. I'm thinking of applying to U.C. Berkeley or S. F. State.*

*It's a gorgeous afternoon. I would LOVE to get out of this house. I want to be up at Foothill Park but I feel too lousy to drive. Jessie and Bambi just left for the mall. Bambi's eyes were plastered with so much goop she looked like a sex-crazed raccoon.*

*I should talk. I look especially lovely. Allow me to describe the vision in the mirror: a yellow bandanna over patchy hair, skin the color of cottage cheese, chapped lips (if I smile, they bleed), flat breasts, and a fat stomach under a stretched-out sweatshirt.*

*I look better than this when I go to school but the overall effect is still pathetic.*

*I talked to Bloomfield at school today. We've been doing quite a bit of that recently. It's too late for us to be anything but friends, but friends is a lot. Friends is plenty.*

*Jessie saw us together and walked by scowling. She looked so funny we laughed. That made her even madder. She went storming off. Bloomfield said, "I get the feeling that your sister doesn't like me."*

*"She holds a grudge," I said. "She thinks you treated me badly."*

*"She's right," he said. "I'm sorry, Helen. I'm sorry about everything."*

*Someday Bloomfield will be a very nice man. He is positively RIFE with possibilities.*

*He said he's been doing a lot of thinking and has decided that the important things in life are: knowing how to make a living, discovering your favorite thing to do (like my writing) and doing it, being considerate of and kind to others, and being able to roll with the punches.*

*Not to mention brushing after every meal, he added. I plan to include that in HTSYL.*

*We talked about graduation, which isn't far away. Everybody worries that their parents will go overboard and do something crazy at the ceremony. Last year Jamie Bonner's parents had a plane fly overhead, trailing a banner that read, WE LOVE YOU, JAMIE! That wouldn't have been bad if the plane had left quickly, but it circled the field for fifteen minutes while Jamie sank lower and lower in her chair. . . . She never showed up at the grad night party.*

*Bloomfield says he just hopes that his father hasn't been drinking or he'll probably jump up and shout, "That's my boy!" when Bloomfield collects his diploma. Mr. Bloomfield is an alcoholic. Bloomfield made that more clear than he ever has before. It wasn't easy for him to talk about it.*

*I may be wrong, but I think Bloomfield wants to ask me to go to the grad night party with him. I got that drift today. I may be wrong, but I think he's afraid to, because of everything that's happened.*

*I may be wrong, but if he doesn't have the nerve I'm going to let him off the hook and ask him.*

## 18

"EVERYBODY'S WAITING, JESS," MY MOTHER SAID, LEANING against the edge of my bed, her arms folded across her chest as if to warm her heart.

"I haven't finished getting dressed," I said. "You better go ahead and eat without me."

I got up and opened my closet door, languidly pawing through the clothes inside.

"Everything's going to be cold," she said.

"That's okay. I'm not really hungry."

She jumped me from behind and spun me around, her face so close I smelled the wine on her breath.

"Are you crazy?" she shouted. "Are you trying to kill yourself? Dear God, what is the matter with this family?"

"Mom, let go of me. You're hurting my arm."

"Do you think I'm going to stand by and let another one

of my babies die? I won't! Do you hear me, Jessie?"

"Of course I hear you. You're yelling in my ear. I'm just not hungry."

"You must think I'm awfully dumb!"

"I don't think you're dumb—"

My mother let go of me and walked to the windows. She stared out into darkness until she caught her breath. "I know you're hurting, honey. We're all hurting. Losing Helen has just about killed me," she said. "But I can't lie down and die. I've got a family that needs me. We really need you too, Jessie. We're sitting at the table, waiting for you—"

"Did you let Bloomfield have Helen's chair?"

"Yes."

"You shouldn't have done that."

"Why not? Helen doesn't sit there anymore." My mother knelt beside the bed where I sat, reaching out to take my hands. "Jessie," she crooned, "can't you come out and play? Don't lock yourself away in your room. Do you want to be like Mrs. Jensen, honey, living in a dream world by herself, waiting for a child who can never come back? If there is a heaven, and Helen can see us, how do you think she feels when we're sad?"

"Oh, Ma." I stood up. "I don't believe in that stuff. Do you think Helen's at a big party with Gram and Gramps, and Mrs. Jensen's kid, and all the people who have ever died? She's gone, Mom! You might as well face it!"

"I have, honey. Now it's up to you." She kissed my forehead and held me close. "People we love become part of who we are. We never really lose them."

"I want to see Helen." My eyes burned with unshed tears.

"Close your eyes and open your heart," my mother murmured. She hugged me, then stepped into the hall. "I want you to join us at the table, Jessie. I've made some of your favorite things: spaghetti and garlic bread and cherry salad."

I've never cared for cherry salad. Helen did.

"I can't, Mom."

"You must," she said. "I'll send Bloomfield up to get you."

"If you do, I'll take off all my clothes."

"I'll tell him. I'm sure he'll be pleased," she said.

I slammed the door. Seconds later he knocked.

"Room service," he announced.

"I'm completely naked."

"Terrific!" He opened the door and barged in. "You lied to me," he said. He was wearing a pair of those glasses with the fake mustache and eyebrows and nose.

"I see you got new glasses. Or is it Halloween?"

"Every day is Halloween around here."

"Tell me about it! My family is so weird! Most mothers are afraid to leave their daughters alone with guys. My mother's practically locking you in the bedroom!"

"She's worried about you, Jess."

"I'm worried about her!"

It was hard to stay mad. He looked ridiculous.

"Can that possibly be a smile or are you snarling at me?"

"A little of both," I said. "You look insane."

"You should see your father."

"He's wearing them, too?" I almost rushed downstairs.

Bloomfield nodded. "Your mother's idea. She thought it would cheer you up. She practically had to hold a gun on your brother."

I laughed, picturing Lucas in those glasses.

"Come on downstairs. They're waiting, Jess."

I shook my head. "They need Helen."

"Nobody expects you to be your sister. They want Jessie back again. Where's that famous sense of humor?"

"Things aren't so funny anymore," I said. "Can I ask you something?"

He braced himself. "I guess."

"Did you ask Helen to go to the grad night party?" I hadn't come to that part in her journal yet. I had been saving the last few pages.

"Yes," Bloomfield said. "She was going to ask me, too."

"Why didn't you ever tell me? I blamed you for being so awful to Helen."

"I was. That part was true," he said. "The rest was between me and Helen."

I sat down on my bed. I needed to think. "Go ahead," I said. "I'll be right down."

"You promise?" He looked skeptical.

I crossed my heart. At that moment, I meant it. Moments ticked into minutes. I locked the door. They were downstairs, waiting. I can only be Jess. She is such a disappointment, weak and childish and petty. Everybody loved Helen best.

Especially me.

Someone tried to open my bedroom door, then pounded on it.

"Jessie," Lucas said, "it's me."

"I'm not coming downstairs."

"Open this door. Open it or I'll break it down!"

"Leave me alone."

"The hell I will! I'm giving you to the count of three. One . . . two . . ."

"Get out of here, Lucas!"

He smashed into the door, again and again. My parents and Bloomfield thundered up the stairs.

"Lucas!" Dad shouted. "What in God's name are you doing?"

"Opening Jessie's door. It's stuck."

"She'll come out of there when she's ready," Mom said.

"Don't count on it, Ma." The door shuddered. "At this rate, she'll die of old age first," Lucas said.

"Lucas, you're upset—"

"Yes, I'm upset, Dad. That's very perceptive. One sister's dead and the other one's dying. It's making me a little touchy!"

"Your dad just—"

"Shut up, Bloomfield. I don't even know why you're here."

"He's here because Mom invited him!" I shouted. "So why don't you shut up, Lucas?"

"Why don't you come out and make me?"

"Lucas, please!"

"Mom, I just want to talk to her, okay? Give us a few minutes alone together. Please."

"It's worth a try," I heard Bloomfield say. He and my parents went downstairs.

"It's you and me, Jess. Open the door," Lucas said. "Nothing bad's going to happen. Open this door or I'll have you for dinner."

"You're scaring me, Lucas."

"I hope so."

"Do you promise you won't hit me?"

"When have I ever hit you?"

"That time at the park, when I was seven. You told me to quit following you—"

"Have I hit you since then?"

"No, but—"

"Open the door or I'll start!"

I let him in. He was wearing those fake glasses. When I laughed he remembered them. He pulled them off and rubbed his face as though he were exhausted.

"Damn it to hell, Jess. Why'd you have to spoil it? Everybody's trying so hard but you."

"Bullshit. Who's the voice of doom? Every time I mention Helen's name you practically run out of the room."

"The hell I do."

"It's true. You and Dad. Everything's always boohoo. Why can't you be happy when we talk about Helen?"

"Too bad I'm not well-adjusted like you. Does your shrink know you won't leave your room?"

"What's the matter, Lucas? Can't you face the facts? When Helen said she loved you, you couldn't say it back! You just sat there like a lump and said, 'Thanks a lot.' "

"Did she tell you that?" He grabbed my arms. "Did she say I didn't love her?"

"No! I read it in her diary!"

My brother groaned as if I'd stabbed him, sinking onto my bed. He covered his face with his hands and moaned, rocking back and forth.

"Lucas, I'm sorry. I didn't mean it. Helen knew you loved her. She said you did. Listen to me, Lucas! It's in her diary! Look, it's right here! I'll read it!"

I'd never told Helen I loved her. And she had never told me. We were children, with all the time in the world for everything that needed to be said and done. We were sisters; we knew we loved each other. We said it in a hundred ways every day, from: "Your slip is showing," to "The phone's for you."

Helen, I love you as much right now as I ever did, and always will.

Lucas uncovered his face. He was crying. I hadn't seen him cry since he was little. His tears dissolved something sharp inside me. My heart cracked open and overflowed, rising in a blinding tide to my eyes.

A long time later, when I could see again, my brother was still beside me.

He said, "I love what you've done to your eyes. You look divine."

"I wouldn't talk if I were you." I reached into the

nightstand and grabbed a box of Kleenex, handing him a few.

"Well, shit," Lucas said. "We've missed dinner. They're probably wondering if we've killed each other. I suppose you want to go see your boyfriend."

"He's not my boyfriend."

"Why did Mom invite him? He was lousy to Helen."

"In a way," I said, "but they made up before she died."

"Did you ever tell her you loved her?" Lucas asked me.

"Not in words," I said, "but she knew. Just like she did with you. You saw what she said in her journal."

Lucas nodded. "I still wish I'd told her."

"Yeah," I said. "Me, too."

He pulled me to my feet. "Let's go face the music."

"In a minute. I have to wash my face."

"Oh, sure. Then you lock yourself in the bathroom and drown yourself in the tub. What am I going to do with you, Jess? I can't let you stay in this house."

"And you can't get me out. It's my problem, Lucas. But I appreciate your concern."

"Then I know you'll appreciate this special offer. On Saturday I'm calling in sick to work. Then you and I are taking a ride to Foothill Park if I have to drive the Impala into your bedroom."

"You will," I said. "I'm scared."

"Scared of what?" He grabbed me. "Scared you're going to freak out? Scared you're going to be hurt? Everybody's scared! And there's a simple explanation: Life is a hair-

raising business! It can kill you! The thing is, you've got
to keep hanging in there! You gotta lives till you dies!"

"You're squishing me, Lucas." He was out of practice in
the hug department.

He let me go. "Shall I send up Romeo?"

"No, I'll be down in a second."

"You better be," he said, "or the car comes through the
door."

I went into the bathroom and washed my face. My eyes
and nose were red. I wondered what my parents and
Bloomfield had been doing while Lucas and I were cussing
and sobbing. Bloomfield had probably fled.

I had to force myself down the stairs. They were sitting
at the dinner table; my parents, my brother, my sister's lost
love, turned toward me like sunflowers and I was the dawn.

"I hope I haven't kept you waiting," I said from behind
my plastic mustache.


I'm in an elevator. It goes up and up. It stops; the doors
slide open with a gasp. I step out onto the shiny white floor.
White walls, endless shiny halls, humming with bright fluo-
rescent lights. A familiar smell, an uneasy mix of ammonia
and flowers. I realize where I am.

I'm at the hospital.

There's no one. Anywhere. The nurse's station is empty.
But the coffee pot is bubbling and the switchboard is lit
with a hundred blinking calls on hold. The windows are
black. The clock reads two.

I start to run. My footsteps ring. The doors that line the corridors are shut. I want to open a door but I'm afraid. My heart is heaving.

A door opens; someone steps into the hall.

It's Helen.

It's Helen! I'm so glad to see her! Happy tears warm my cheeks. She looks wonderful in a loose white gown. Her hair is a dark shawl across her back.

She smiles at me. We rush into each other's arms.

"Jessie," she says, "what are you doing here?" She sounds more like Mom than like Helen, as if she's grown up since the last time I'd seen her, and I'm still a child. I feel safe.

"Helen, you have to come home right away."

"It's late," she says gently. "You should be in bed."

"I can't sleep. I get so scared, Helen."

"Scared of what?" She searches my face.

"I'm afraid I can't find you." I feel silly saying it, with Helen right here beside me.

"You always find me." She laughs softly, then stares at my bare feet. "Where are your shoes?"

I can't remember. "I guess I left them at home."

"You really should have your shoes on, Jessie. Mom would have a fit."

I tug Helen's hand. "I hate this place. We have to leave before they all come back."

"I can't come with you, Jess." She puts her hand on my arm. Her fingernails are like opals.

I start to cry. I can't help it. Helen holds me close.

"Don't be sad," she says. "This is only a dream."
My cheek is on her chest. I can feel her heart beating.
"Are you sure?" I say. "It seems so real."
"Of course it's a dream. We're not really in a hospital."
"Then where are we? Helen?" My arms are empty. My eyes are blind. "Please don't leave me!"
"I'm right here, Jessie."
I hear the words in my mind. My heart opens like a rose. I feel at peace.
I walk down the empty hall and step into the elevator. The hospital is only a dream. Helen and I are free to leave.

## 19

MAY 31

*I have found the dress I'm going to wear to grad night. It was in the window of a little shop at Town & Country Village.*

*It's blue, lit with light like the morning sky; simple yet elegant, too. I put it on layaway and will bail it out before the 15th.*

*I'm afraid to bring it home 'cause then Jessie will know I'm going with Bloomfield and she'll have a fit. She'll tell me he's a jerk, I'm too good for him, etc., that I have no business going out with him After Everything He Did.*

*It's my life, not hers. I don't care what she says!*

*Which is why I haven't brought home the dress.*

*Bloomfield was so cute when he asked me. I started smiling before he even said a thing, 'cause I could tell. We were standing in front of the house after school, Jessie glaring daggers out the bedroom window at his back, so I made a point of acting extra entranced.*

*Bloomfield said, "Uh, Helen, there's something I have to ask you."*

*I started cracking up.*

*"What's so funny?" he said.*

*"Your face. I mean—"*

*"What about my face?" He was laughing, too.*

*"When you're serious you get this little tuck around your mouth."*

*"Like this?"*

*"Exactly." I couldn't quit laughing.*

*"Well, what about you? Here's my impression of Helen: Me: 'There's something I have to ask you.' Helen: 'Your face is so funny! Ha ha ha!'"*

*He reeled around the front lawn, clutching his sides. I was gasping for air.*

*"This is serious!" he shouted.*

*"I'm listening, Bloomfield! Seriously, seriously!"*

*"I want to go to the grad night party with you!"*

*"I know you do! I thought you'd never ask!"*

*"How can I, when you're acting like a lunatic?"*

*I haven't even told Mom, 'cause she'll get so excited and of course she'll tell Jessie, who'll have a cow. You're Making a Terrible Mistake, etc. I can hear it now.*

*On the fifteenth day of June I will graduate from high school. My life is changing. And so am I.*

*And so is Bloomfield.*

*I just hope I don't feel lousy then. I'm fighting another cold. My resistance is so low I'm mugged by any nasty bug passing through.*

*And I wish that all my hair would suddenly grow back, luxuriant as bunny fur. The wig is not so bad (not so good, either). I wear it with a bandanna, which accomplishes two purposes: 1) it keeps my hair from blowing off when a truck roars by, and 2) it hides the fakiest part of the wig—the part. What hangs down my back looks like my old hair used to, if you don't look too hard.*

*I'm wondering what to wear with my grad night dress. A bandanna would be tacky. A cowboy hat? I saw some sequined berets at Macy's. Pretty snazzy. And expensive, but why the heck not? I don't graduate from high school every day. Thank God.*

*I'm glad Bloomfield and I are friends again.*

*It's better this time. It's more relaxed. We know for a fact that we're both human. I ain't a princess and he sure ain't the prince.*

*We talk a lot more than we used to.*

*It's funny how things come back sometimes, when you think they're gone forever. This winter the yard looked completely dead. Now everything's in bloom. The other day Mom and I planted iris bulbs. Hard to believe they're full of flowers.*

*Lucas says the band that will play at grad night is terrible; a bunch of Top Forty punks. Their name is Shout but he calls them the Sell-Outs. Fortunately, the music at school dances is too loud to really hear.*

*Sara Rose wanted me to come out and play today but I didn't have the juice. I hate to disappoint her but I had to take a nap. I felt better when I woke up. Then Bambi came by to shock me with her new hair style: Her head looks and feels like a peach. We got out the Ouija board for a while, but all it would say was EAT MY SHORTS, so we gave up on the future. Then I listened to her and Jess have this really stupid (and hilarious) argument. I secretly taped it and played it back, which made them both so mad!*

*B: Well, you said you liked him.*

*J: No, I didn't.*

*B: Yes, you did. You told Susie and she told me.*

*J: I never told Susie.*

*B: Well, she said you did.*

*J: Are you calling me a liar?*

*B: Susie's not a liar.*

*J: She is if she says I said I liked him. I think he's the biggest jerk in the world. Well, the second biggest jerk.*

*B: Are you talking about me?*

*J: I never said that.*

*B: If I'm such a jerk, then how come I'm the one with all the boyfriends, not you?*

*J: Cuz they're jerks, too!*

*B: Oh, listen who's talking!*

*J: Yeah, you!*

*B: No, you!*

*J: No, you're the one who's talking.*

*B: Then who just said, 'No, you're the one who's talking'?*

*J: You!*

*They sounded like a comedy act. Sometimes they don't like each other at all; they're just a habit.*

*My stomach is urpy. I should eat something but it might come right back up. In a while Mom and Dad are taking me to see Dr. Yee. Just a checkup, then we'll do some shopping.*

*I would like to tell them about Bloomfield (and my beautiful dress!) but only if they'll promise not to tell Jessie. I'd prefer to tell her myself. Perhaps via skywriting during the graduation ceremony. . . .*

## 20

I WENT TO THE HOSPITAL THE LAST TIME WITH HELEN.
That's what really happened. I did not stay home.

I almost didn't go. I had a science test the next day but
I didn't feel like studying. Besides, Helen needed cheering
up. She'd been feeling pretty low.

We thought it was a cold. Or the flu or something.
We weren't blind. Our eyes were closed.

It was no big deal, just another hospital run. The transfu-
sions made Helen feel better. Everybody noticed, and nobody mentioned, that she was going days earlier than
scheduled.

Dad carried Helen out to the car. Usually she put up a
fuss when he babied her. This time she didn't say a word,
just wrapped her arms around his neck.

When we got to the hospital, nurses took her to her

room. I wandered off and bought a *Cosmopolitan*. It was full of sappy articles that would make Helen laugh, like: "Kiss Your Flabby Fanny Good-bye!"

When I got back, Helen wasn't in her room. Mom and Dad were gone. I couldn't find a nurse. Dr. Yee was being paged. I started running down the hall. Dad found me. He said, "Hurry, Jessie."

Everything speeded up. Dad pushed me through a door. It was Helen's new room. There were no other patients. The room was so quiet. I'd expected confusion. There was only one nurse, and Dr. Yee, and Mom. Helen was in the bed, unconscious.

Dr. Yee touched her arm. Helen murmured something. It sounded like, "Oh, shit."

Dr. Yee said: "Helen, we're ordering blood."

Helen opened her eyes and said, "Save it for someone who needs it."

Doctors floated in and out. So did Helen. She was having trouble breathing. They gave her a shot and turned her on her side. Mom and Dad stroked her hair. Helen whispered something. It was "Jessie" or "Help me."

Then my sister hemorrhaged internally and died.

The nurse was crying. Mom and Dad were crying. Helen was lying there. I ran out of the hospital and got in the car, and when my parents found me, I said, "Don't talk." All the way home I thought: HelenHelenHelen, as if her name could protect me.

We got to the house—I burst past Lucas. He's shouting,

"What's wrong? What's the matter?"

I ran up to our bedroom and locked the door. Then I cried and cried and cried and cried, until my head throbbed and my jaw ached and my eyes were bloody and raw. Then I stopped and I thought, My heart has died. God can't hurt me anymore.

But the heart is as tough as an iris bulb. The flowers are blooming and Sara Rose is like a bird, calling outside my bedroom window, "Jess-sie-ee! Jess-sie-ee! Can you come out and play?"

Not today, I say. Maybe sometime soon.

## 21

JUNE 9

*I don't feel good. I am sick of this feeling. I am missing the last days of school.*

*Yesterday I went for a while, but I had to come home. I felt crummy.*

*I get so mad at myself. Why can't I transcend my body? Millions of people all over the world are suffering more than me, yet they keep on plugging away every day.*

*Helen Castle, Queen of the Complainers, says: Woe is me!*

*Bloomfield called awhile ago. His voice is like ginger ale. The minute I hear him, I start to feel better. Probably 'cause I'm laughing so much.*

*Mom just brought me some toast and tea so I'll have something to throw up. Usually I love this kind of tea, but today it smells like socks and closets.*

*Outside, an orange dragonfly embroiders the summer day. If I ever have a daughter I will name her Summer. Or Autumn or Spring.*

*I will not name her Winter. Or Gidget or Bambi or Bernice.*

*I want to go get my blue dress today.*

*Oh shit, I am going to throw up.*

## 22

IT'S FRIDAY AFTERNOON. I SHOULD BE IN SCHOOL. I WISH I WAS. That's the weird part. I kind of miss seeing everybody.

Even Dr. Shubert. She called today to see how I'm doing.

"What're you up to these days, Jessie?"

"About five foot eight," I said.

I told her that I still can't leave the house.

Dad's at work, Mom's gone to the store. My school work is done. I'm bored with TV. There's nothing on but soap operas and they can't hold a bubble to real life.

Bloomfield is coming by tonight. He says we'll either play Yahtzee or bicker, whichever I'd prefer. I told him not to bother, but I'm glad he's coming over. Bambi never comes by anymore. (If I'd known this would work, I would've flipped out sooner.)

Lucas says he's taking me to Foothill Park tomorrow if

he has to lock me in the trunk of his car.

Great, I say, then I won't have to watch you drive.

I'm not going to worry about tomorrow right now. It's almost three o'clock. Way down the block, I see Mrs. Jensen heading for the bus stop. Sara Rose will be by soon, as she is every day, inviting me to come out and play. She doesn't know the meaning of the word discouragement. Or of lots of other words, for that matter.

Although it's only March, the air is warm. The windows are open and the curtains are stirring. Lucas is playing his acoustic guitar. It's a song I've never heard before.

He stops and restarts it, and after awhile I realize it's something being born. It's not like the tunes Lucas usually writes, with their fast, brash riffs and their bluesy chords. This melody draws me out of my bedroom and down the hall to his door.

He's sitting on the bed, bent over his guitar, his face tilted up as if he's listening to the sky. Suddenly I know what has drawn me to the song.

"It's Helen," I say.

Lucas looks at me and nods. Then he is lost inside the music.

I listen to his gift describe our sister: dark and light and sweet and warm; funny and loving and bright and wise; a daughter, a sister, a child, a woman; a sorceress in a medieval forest teeming with the creatures who inhabited her poems; sprites and phoenixes and jewel-eyed mermaids and unicorns nursing their young.

I see Helen, at Foothill Park, running across the bright green hills that ripen into golden waves as she passes across them like summer.

I see Helen smiling, on the beach with Bloomfield, in love with him forever.

I see my sister, and I feel her with us, in the heart of Lucas's art.

He pauses, frowning, then begins the song again, creating, discovering, remembering.

Outside, Sara Rose is calling.

I lean out my window. She smiles up at me, bright as her scarlet sweater.

"Jessie, can you come out and play?" she says.

And this time Jessie says yes.

## 23

JUNE 12

*I've had the best idea for a story! I'm so excited! I got the idea from that paper I did for Ms. Tormey, the one about the phoenix and the concept of rebirth. It's about this girl who thinks she's dead but she's not; she's really in a coma, in this other world.*

*It sounds so sappy when I put it like that. I better quit blabbing and write it. But if I say so myself, it's going really well.*

*And if you don't believe me, take my word for it!*

*Feeling better today. Jessie made me lunch and she made me laugh. She's so pretty when she smiles. I told her that. As usual, she felt obliged to make a face, but I think she might've heard me, for once.*

*I invited her to come with me tomorrow when I pick up my blue dress. I didn't get around to mentioning Bloomfield yet. Why wreck her terrific mood?*

*I'm supposed to see Dr. Yee next week but am feeling much improved.*

*Am trying to be a nicer person lately; not teasing my brother even though it's such fun; or getting mad at Jessie (grrrrr) when she slobs up our room. And letting Mom and Dad know how much I love them.*

*And brushing after every meal, as Bloomfield would add.*

*I'm trying to live each day as though it were my last. Not because of the Big C, but because you never know, really. Today is all we have. And even though I feel lousy sometimes, I still love life with ALL MY HEART.*

*Wellllll, maybe not every single second. But usually.*

*I want to show that love in my writing. But I can never quite say what I mean. Maybe life's too big to fit on paper. Or maybe my pencil's too short.*

*I'd like to be able to make readers laugh and cry; to reach across the page and say, Hey, we're alive! I want to show the courage of fathers and mothers who bring forth babies who brave the maze of childhood; learning to crawl, standing up, oops, falling, starting over, getting up, going on, finding love, losing hope, enduring pain and disappointment; believing that happiness is just around the corner, if we don't give up, if we keep moving forward—*

*There is so much I want to say.*